CAVES OF THE
RUST BELT

CAVES OF THE RUST BELT

Ohio Stories

Joe Kapitan

Tortoise Books
Chicago, IL

FIRST EDITION 2018

Caves of the Rust Belt: Ohio Stories © *2018 by Joe Kapitan*

All rights reserved under International and Pan-American Copyright Convention

Published in the United States by Tortoise Books. (www.tortoisebooks.com)

ISBN-10: 1-948954-00-1
ISBN-13: 978-1-948954-00-6

There are no unsacred places; there are only sacred places and desecrated places.

Wendell Berry, "How to Be a Poet"

Table of Contents

Caves of the Rust Belt

Don't believe me if you want, but the hole just appeared one night. It was late June; I know because the Lake Erie mayflies had already swarmed and mated and died. Also, it may have been raining a little. But by morning, gone were the aboveground pool and Mom's favorite lilac. In their place lay a gaping hole.

The fire department came and roped it off with yellow warning tape. Then came the news cameras. Dad ended up on the evening broadcast, in his bathrobe. He said we were lucky we weren't all sucked down asleep in our beds. He looked more alive than he had in months, since before Ford closed Casting Plant #2 on Brookpark and sent so many dads home to daytime television, idled.

The geologists from Case Western came next. They set up some fancy equipment on the rim of the hole. The mayor stood nearby, concerned. Ours was the third sinkhole that week. The first one took out the old gym at Perry Elementary—the one that closed in the consolidation. The second opened up across Route 23 and swallowed a dump truck full of crushed concrete; rubble from the abandoned Con-Agra grain elevators that were coming down.

Mom kept right on going like there was no hole, because that was her. She got us our pancakes in the morning and dropped us at Aunt Sara's so she wouldn't be late to work again at Kmart. One more time, said her boss, and you're out. There's ten more waiting to take your place.

Dad set up a lawn chair next to the warning tape. He talked to all the experts. He found out about karst limestone and water tables and how the earth below us was being eaten away a little at a time, while we weren't paying attention. He talked to the drillers, the guys from Oklahoma who were up in our parts fracking the shale for natural gas and always looking for easier ways in. He talked with archaeologists from the Natural History Museum about Pre-Cambrian and Cambrian layers. He talked about all this stuff over pancakes at dinner, waving his fork in the air while Mom washed dishes. We gotta go downward to go upward, he kept saying. He couldn't sleep the first night after the hole.

On the second night, he went in. Snuck right in.

He climbed back out the next day around noon, filthy with mud, carrying Haley's inflatable turtle from our pool in one hand and some animal skull in the other that looked like it came from a huge, nasty cat. Haley hugged him hard. The curator of the museum happened to be there at the time. He took one look at the skull and promised to pay Dad $2,000 for it. Mom hugged the curator hard.

By nightfall, word had spread. A huge crowd had gathered on our lawn: men with too much time on their hands; women with too little; kids with nothing. They packed themselves in tighter and tighter, jumped and stomped, pressured the earth, hoping to break through.

Letter from a Welder's Son, Unsent

Have you discovered yet, as I have, that the sins of a welder's son eventually find you as sparks and flashes in troubled sleeps, as smoldering apparitions cast in ragged light?

This one lingers. This particular one is 1974, a June day, the last day of sixth grade. A tall-haired teacher pins up one of those Cold-War-era civil defense maps showing probable nuclear targets in America; the maps with the overlapping red circles covering all the major urban areas on both coasts, but not too many in the Northwest or in the West where the cowboys and the militia-types live (Russians, apparently, don't find either of them threatening in the least). She points to the circle that covers the northern edge of Ohio. We're right here at the edge of this circle, she says. If a Soviet missile strikes here (stabs Cleveland with her right index), we'll probably survive the initial blast, but we'll die a slow and painful death from radioactive particle poisoning. A bell rings. Have a safe summer, she says. The classroom drains, and a boy walks home alone, baseball cap pulled down tight on his head, for the sole purpose of hiding his vacant scalp. As far as radiation and hair are concerned, the teacher had warned them, fall-out means FALL OUT. So, given that, would everyone around him, as they vomited their blood and shed their skin, realize that he was simply a little better prepared for the inevitable? Then again, in a time of terminal sicknesses, wouldn't his condition become irrelevant? Wouldn't falling missiles and their mushroom-cloud blooms render all conditions and their disguises irrelevant?

There is a father, already back from work when the boy arrives home; implausible for a weekday. The father sits on the front porch, cold beer clamped to his forehead, not acknowledging the boy. The father stares out beyond the porch, out over the carefully manicured lawns greened to the level suburban consensus deemed appropriate for the representation of stability. Attached to the front porch is the white colonial that cannot sustain five children. Five is three too many, according to the father's own brutal math muttered late at night—but mercifully, the boy has never overheard the father put any names to the excess.

Through the front door and hallway is the kitchen, and in the kitchen, the refrigerator and the stove and the mother, all three exhausted. The refrigerator's compressor is failing, and the oven nestled beneath the stovetop doesn't heat, and the boy watches the mother closely to see if what people say is true about breakdowns and threes.

It is the mother in the kitchen, peeling potatoes, who explains the news to the boy. The boy knows of his father's job as a union welder at the Ford plant on Brookpark, but what you don't understand, Son, the mother tells the boy, is that cars run on oil, exactly the stuff that the Arabs have decided to stop selling to the West. It is a simple economic formula that she recites to him: empty refineries equal empty automobile assembly lines equal the father on the front porch at three in the afternoon on a Friday, looking like he is going to dismember the next Muslim-looking person or unfortunately swarthy-skinned Greek he sees.

The boy goes back outside and sits next to the father. Maybe now we can build a tree house together, says the boy.

Maybe, mumbles the father, more to the beer than the boy.

Here comes July, then, and look—over there is the new-fangled electronic thermometer sign on the National City Bank building downtown, registering triple digits, and now the summer begins to boil over. Now it starts, with an innocent conversation between the mother and Mrs. Mechanic from two doors down. Mrs. Mechanic, mother of Gary, the obligatory neighborhood runt and ubiquitous abuse magnet. Mrs. Mechanic, inconspicuous wife of the Mechanic, Gary's rarely seen father, who sometimes emerges from their house at dusk to lovingly tinker with his suped-up, shit-brown 1973 Ford Gran Torino sitting up on cinder blocks in the driveway. The remainder of the Mechanic's existence is spent in his garage workshop, behind a garage door kept permanently closed, surrounded by random machinery, and somewhere amidst that machinery might be Gary's rumored, mechanical half-brother the Robot, who (according to a majority of local teenagers polled) is constructed of equal parts lawn mower engine and dime-store mannequin.

Here is the boy again, sunburned and freshly paroled from summer camp. He hears the sound of hammers coming from behind the house. The hammers, he discovers, are swung by the father and his laid-off union buddies, who are loud and unsteady and just finishing the railing on a tree house.

It's done? says the boy.

What, you don't you like it? asks the father.

It doesn't look like what I drew, says the boy.

But it's done, says the father.

Can we put in a little elevator to lift things? asks the boy.

Maybe some other time, answers the father.

The father and his buddies slap each other's backs and gather their tools. The boy climbs the ladder into the tree house and sweeps out the empty beer cans with his forearm.

Now there is Gary, alone, watching this scene from the security of his own backyard. Gary is being harassed several times a week now, mercilessly attacked for everything from his stiff-legged walk, to his wearing long pants even on the most searing summer days, to the fact that his father, the Mechanic, seems to care more about leaf springs than offspring. In fact, the boy's mother (the exhausted one) is the only one on the street who is at all civil to the entire Mechanic family. The boy has even noticed his mother and

Mrs. Mechanic having conversations. Actual conversations, for Christ's sake. Like the morning Mrs. Mechanic complains to the exhausted mother about the inflation of grocery prices due to the Oil Crisis, and the mother, lost in a moment of neighborly commiseration, lets it slip about the lay-offs at the auto plant and the unemployment checks. That's all it takes—gossip is passed around that neighborhood like a joint amongst the stoners gathered in their hazy, Army-jacketed scrum behind the high school gym.

Now here is Gary once more, still freshly wounded from a spectacular public shaming two days earlier. He had been cruising down the middle of the street displaying his no-hands skills on his Mechanic-made banana-seat bike, when the whole thing disintegrated out from under him. There wasn't a single nut and bolt left touching. So, there he was, Gary, flat on his back in the street atop a carpet of bike parts, and the boy pointing at him and laughing his ass off. A crowd of young hecklers gathered immediately, sensing opportunity. Gary picked himself up, scarlet-faced, and did his best to storm back to his house, but it came off more like the waddle of a murderous penguin. He stayed holed up in his house, undoubtedly stewing in the poisonous broth of his own malicious thoughts, until the morning he happened to walk into his kitchen, just in time to overhear the boy's mother tell Mrs. Mechanic how you don't know what humble feels like until you're cashing unemployment checks.

And this here, this must be August now, because the carefully manicured lawns are a desiccated brown, and their illusion of order has disappeared along with the rain. The father, the mother, the boy, and his four siblings (some of them excess) are now infamous up and down the street as the family that is barely surviving courtesy of Uncle Sam's pseudo-welfare (gasp!) program. Gary has made it his personal mission to ensure the whole neighborhood knows about it. Now it is the boy's turn to hole up and stew. So, stew he does.

The boy plunks himself down on the front porch, still warm with day heat, and sulks silently while the father drinks a few wish-it-was-after-work Miller High Lifes with the guys from the auto plant. They have taken to congregating on the porch. Big Rudy is there, and Jimmy Ippolito with the usual unlit cigar clenched in his teeth, and Stan Jaworski, too. The father calls the boy out, makes him speak up about what's bothering him, and the boy does, right in front of the other guys, right up through the unemployment check part. Stan just shakes his head. Jimmy Ippolito stares at some tiny object embedded in the concrete. Big Rudy pretends to notice, for the first time, one of the old Marine Corps tattoos on his massive forearm. The father finds his granite face, the one usually reserved for the in-laws. He stands up and stalks toward the driveway.

The boy says, Dad, where are you going?

The father says, going to talk to the Mechanic about his boy.

When he comes back ten minutes later, he doesn't look any better, and perhaps worse. Stan Jaworski suggests maybe they should all leave. The father says, no, you guys stick around a while, one more beer and it'll be dark. He sends the boy to bed.

Here is the sun rising the next morning, and the boy awakens to the sound of murmuring voices. From his bedroom window, he can see that a sizable crowd has gathered in front of the Mechanics' place. Now the boy leaves his house to get a closer look, and then he sees what they are pointing at: the shit-brown 1973 Ford Gran Torino, resting upside-down on the grass next to the Mechanics' driveway, with its wheel-less axles pointing at the sky, looking for all the world like a dead dung beetle.

Here's the big question: the boy should probably leave the unfortunate Mechanics alone after that episode, shouldn't he? Isn't that enough? But it isn't, somehow, and he doesn't. He can't. He is convinced that they have one more concealed closet to be opened, with one more embarrassing skeleton in it, and that closet is the Mechanic's garage, and that skeleton's name is the Robot.

So, here is the side door of the Mechanic's garage, left unlocked one evening, and now the boy slips inside, crouching behind a drill press, the pupils of his eyes slowly growing accustomed to the dim lighting. There is a clearing in the center of the garage, the only place one could actually move around in the entire place, and in the clearing rests a chair, and oxygen and acetylene tanks with hoses connected to a portable welding machine, and two small sculptures made of metal latticework that are wider at their tops than at their bottoms. As the boy's eyes adjust more fully to the half-light of a single dangling bulb, the sculptures begin to take on the appearance of legs. Human legs. See, now, how the latticed frames are actually welded cages, each contoured into the shape of a human leg, and each of the cages is separated from itself at the knee joints and again at the ankle joints to allow movement, and within the cages are various assemblies of pulleys and hinges and cables and springs. At the tops of each leg are harnesses, designed for attachment—for attachment, no doubt, to the rest of the Robot.

So, I was right after all, the boy thinks with satisfaction. First, he calculates, I'll find out where they hide him, and then I'll come back later with a camera, after they put the legs on, and take some Polaroids. So, who cares about my dad's unemployment checks, he'll say to the other kids, check out these Polaroids. And you guys were only half-right, he'll say to the local teenagers, just look at those Polaroids. I don't see any lawn mower engine, do you?

The door between the house and garage opens, shooting blinding light into the garage, and the boy shrinks into shadows to avoid detection. The Mechanic is first through the doorway, followed by his son, and they shut the door behind them, returning the garage to near-darkness. They pick their way through piles of machinery to the clearing in the center of the garage. They stop in front of the legs.

They're finished! exclaims Gary, his eyes sparkling across the dim workshop.

What do you think? asks the Mechanic.

They look just like the ones I drew, says Gary.

I did my best, replies the Mechanic.

Is it time to try them out? asks Gary, excitedly.

Yes, it's time, answers the Mechanic.

Now, the motionless boy crouching near the side door is straining to see over the drill press, to see where the rest of the Robot's legless torso is hidden, but the Mechanic makes no motion indicative of retrieval. Instead, Gary struggles now to undo his belt, and drops his pants to his ankles. His underwear is white, and so is the pale skin of his meager thighs, down to the very point where the brown leather begins. From there, leather straps crisscross both his legs at mid-thigh, fastened by a series of small buckles, and below that, below the unnaturally blunt ends of his biology, all else is metallurgy.

Gary sits down on the edge of the chair and attacks the buckles on one thigh, while the Mechanic kneels in front of him and loosens those on the other.

The boy, still hidden, still watching, now dizzy, reaches for the drill press to steady himself.

Gary asks the Mechanic: Dad, will these new ones help me walk better?

The Mechanic stops his unbuckling and looks at his son, touches his arm. I hope so, Buddy, he says, I sure hope so.

The Mechanic finishes removing both of the artificial limbs, and at the sight of about half of Gary suddenly gone, the boy's balance falters and he tumbles backward into galvanized trash cans. The Mechanic shouts and jumps to his feet, but Gary, momentarily confined to the chair, can only manage the shouting part, and both stare wild-eyed at the boy, who somehow scrambles to his feet and escapes out the side door.

Now the boy runs, runs past his own white colonial, runs past a dozen more houses, runs until he feels his dinner climbing up his throat. It is dark already, and his vision blurs. He stops, falls to all fours in some unknown neighbor's petunia bed, and lets his meal loose into the mulch. Now he spits out the remnants, several times, but it doesn't help much. He can still taste bile, mixed up with the constant metallic tinge left in his mouth from the latest round of chemo. He can still taste tears.

He still can.

Answer me this: how else can I extinguish the arcing, still-burning trails of these phantoms, unless I revisit an abandoned truth grown restless in its shallow grave? How else, unless I stop pretending that the one boy isn't me, and the other isn't you?

There are only two weeks left of summer break now, and Dad has been called back to work at the auto plant, so I spend most of those two weeks up in the tree fort, trying to figure out the elevator on my own. You, to your credit, never say another word about the unemployment check business—your détente, I would realize later. You expect me to do the same with that loose thread of yours I hold. But this is back then, after all, the Seventies, the decade purloined by the fear-mongers and chest-thumpers and the pre-empters, and so I pummel you one more time, in the mud under the monkey bars. Remember? I want to pull my punches, but I can't, since they are all gathered around, watching me and my fists and you and your mud-bloody face with such hungry, demanding eyes. You cry, and the other kids laugh, and when they ask me what part of you they should work over, your secret is launched from my mouth before I can even register my tongue on the button.

A Sort of Theology

Gunny does better with his legs removed. He stands them up in front of him, on the corner of 12th and Prospect, and against them props the cardboard sign that reads "Please Help a Vet." With prostheses on, he's a bum; with them detached, a tragic/heroic bum. He tells passersby of the three-way trade that sent his first legs to Al Qaida in return for one used explosive and a Marine Purple Heart. The change rattles as it's tossed into the sockets where his stumps fit in. Usually, after three days, Gunny has enough to eat for a week. After six days, enough to visit Marisol.

Gunny thinks it ironic that Marisol, the failing prostitute, smokes too much; and when she does, the hand that holds the smoldering cigarette to her mouth meets the scar tissue that forms the furthest hemisphere of her face. Eduardo did that, back in San Juan. Jealous Eduardo, and some kerosene, and yet another cigarette, and Marisol had fled with her nostrils full of her own charred flesh, carrying nothing but seed that was not Eduardo's.

Gunny places the cash on the shelf next to the plaster Guadalupe, and sits on the edge of the bed to undo the straps. Marisol finishes her cigarette. Her baby is still sleeping. They make love in the manner they've managed to cobble together, and their moans are gauze across the faces of his wounded comrades, and the bedsprings lull her flames quiet until both bind and seep into their own neglected corner of the world, bodiless and thus woundless, taking years with them, and for a time, there is nothing left in their universe but the two ends, the bomb and the baby. No steps between, only bared mechanism, mathematical clarity. The bomb feeds the baby.

Summer Break Notes, Defiance, Ohio

June blog post: "Three of the seven funerals occurred on the same day, a Saturday in May meant more for weddings, bowties constricting necks, dark clothing absorbing sun, humidity balling up in armpits and condensing into tiny private downpours. Times were staggered so the entire community could toss roses into each of the holes (except, perhaps the shooter's) and stand on the dewy grass of three different cemeteries and try to remember/then forget/then remember; a cycle called coping, or closure, depending on the viewpoints of the various professionals providing grief counseling."[i]

Sophomore Brianna Horovec was shot in the neck from behind as she ate Greek yogurt from a Tupperware. She did not know the shooter, but did have red hair, hair similar (from behind) to the shooter's ex-girlfriend. [ii]

Special Education Instructor Eugene Brodsky will be honored in perpetuity by the creation of the Eugene Brodsky Ordinary Heroes Scholarship Fund, awarded to one deserving senior each year. The winning student must characterize the selflessness exhibited by the late Mr. Brodsky, and "the willingness to act in difficult situations when others are paralyzed with fear or cower beneath desks." [iii]

A public meeting held on July 21st at the Senior Center did not result in a clear-cut direction for the concept of a memorial. A request by the shooter's family to donate money to the project in their son's name was vehemently rejected. Alternative ideas for the funds, such as hiring additional school security officers, were also discussed. [iv]

In a July poll conducted by *The Defiance County Times*, 93% of respondents felt less safe than they did a year ago. [v]

City Council recently approved, via a special August session, an additional $17,000 to cover the cost of full-time police protection at the family home of the shooter. [vi]

"We'll get through this," said Mayor Jim Showalter, while judging the Fourth of July rib burn-off. [vii] "We can't let this change who we are."

[i] This year, all incoming freshmen at Defiance High School will be assigned a mandatory grief counselor and required to meet with their counselor once each semester, in accordance with the district's new Pre-Trauma Initiative.

[ii] The installation of metal detectors at all school entrances will be completed before the first day of classes in late August, reports District Superintendent Denise Manningham. Security officers, who will now carry live firearms (see below), must use a security entrance consisting of two doors with cipher locks.

[iii] The inaugural Brodsky scholarship winner, Jake Andriucci, varsity wrestler, is nearing the completion of his physical therapy and is expected to walk normally by the time he starts classes at Kent State University. His surgeon, Cleveland Clinic Dr. Leo Kleinhenz, credits Jake's superior physical conditioning for his amazing recovery.

[iv] Subsequently, the Memorial Steering Committee met behind closed doors and approved the transfer of funds to the school district, to be used for the purchase of new Beretta 9-millimeter handguns for school security officers. "A pretty

statue won't make anyone safer," explained Committee Chair Maryanne Zimmerman.

[v] Main Street Firearms has reported a 37% increase in sales over this time last year.

[vi] Address: 574 Russett Drive.

[vii] The annual fireworks show has been cancelled indefinitely.

The Basic Problem with Interior Renovation

Me, entrepreneur of necessity, down to one last desperate idea, and suddenly I was spending the hottest afternoon of an entire summer toiling fifty feet in the air, fifty feet closer than my onlookers to the searing late-August sun. I wedged my boots against temporary nailers, leaned into the thirty-degree slope and scraped up decades worth of old roofing, perspiration raining from my nose and sunglasses, sore shoulders plowing again and again through three layers of worn-out asphalt shingles and one layer of ancient tarpaper beneath, down to the original roof structure. My forearms pulsed, cramped from hours of gripping, no longer able to grasp the handle of the scraper. I sat propped against a warped brick chimney to rest, cramming myself into the last remaining sliver of shade, the sweat now tracing channels down my neck and chest, and waited for the rigid claws my hands had become to loosen just enough to twist open the lid of my water jug. It was good to be working. It was crucial to be seen working.

+++

Old mansions like that one were built long before anyone ever conceived of plywood, so the roof sheathing beneath me was the typical handiwork of early nineteenth-century carpenters: solid two-by planking. Eighty percent of it was still in good shape. The areas that had caved in had been shored up and replaced as needed. There was still some rot in the valleys that I had to remove, probably water-damaged from gutter back-up, and just the day before, I'd tackled a section near the main ridge that was all tunneled through with carpenter ants. When I pried that section of ridge loose, they had exploded outward in a frenzied tide. The queen rested in the middle of her chaos, her pale and oblong abdomen too swollen with eggs to move. I spread her out flat with the scraper blade, the contents of her egg sac wetting the damaged wood with slime. No malice, just precaution.

That was my first week of work on the Hollensbee place. Rule Number One: proper interior renovations always start at the roof. To most, that's an oxymoron; it smacks of the sort of lie told by storm-chasing con artists with vinyl signs slapped to the sides of their rusted pick-up trucks, the kind that combine up-sell talk with an accent born three states further south ("Yessir, you can spend money all you want on the inside, but unless you fix them roof leaks, you're pissin' down your own well"), the kind that ask for two-thirds of the cost up front as they smile a crooked mouthful of gaps at you. But if you tell them it's true, with a straight face, they'll think you know what you're talking about. They'll sense that you're legit—that you can tell first-hand what it feels like to have fine plasterwork ruined by an unexpected summer storm that tore through town in less than twenty minutes and left tarps ripped loose and flapping in the wind. Here's what I tell them: a man tends to remember lessons like that, the ones paid for out of his own wallet. After that, a man makes sure there's purpose in everything he does.

+++

I couldn't understand, at first, why anyone in town would want the old Hollensbee place leveled. Wasn't this Hollensbee the Abolitionist we were talking about? Hollensbee the Liberator, who survived an attack by Confederate mercenaries who'd crossed the Ohio, looking to return runaways and collect the generous bounties offered by the plantation owners? The account I'd heard since childhood went something like this:

On a rainy night in the waning days of autumn, with James Buchanan in the White House and fresh news arriving of John Brown's raid at Harpers Ferry, Hollensbee received word from abolitionist sympathizers in town that a small band of southerners had begun to appear in darkened corners of local establishments, seated at rear tables, inquiring about him. Hollensbee rode straight to his cellar and ordered the former slaves hiding there (four men, two women, six children) to chain their wrists and ankles to the walls. A fifth man, a teenager named Bartholomew, was told to hide beneath the stairs with a shotgun. Hollensbee went back upstairs, to wait. Just before midnight, without warning, mercenaries kicked in the front door and searched the house top to bottom. They put a revolver to Hollensbee's head and told him to unlock the cellar door. Hollensbee explained that it was a simple misunderstanding; he'd recently captured two families of Negroes that had just forded the Ohio River at Portsmouth and fallen for his ruse about the Underground Railroad. Hollensbee said he was planning to return them himself. The mercenaries descended the cellar stairs and found the blacks in chains and irons. The southerners began to argue with Hollensbee over ransoms. He'd get no cut of their bounties. Hollensbee protested. One of the mercenaries leveled a rifle to Hollensbee's chest just before an explosion tore through the wooden stairs. Shotgun pellets shredded the southerners. Hollensbee went down, too, buckshot peppering in his right leg. He wrapped his belt around his thigh to slow the bleeding. He gave his ring of keys to Bartholomew. The freed slaves escaped north, to Michigan. The southerners, to a man, died there in the cellar, their bodies burned. Hollensbee lived, but would never walk right again.

This was the Hollensbee of the history texts, and of the white population of Athens, and of most of the black population as well. Schoolchildren at Warren G. Harding Elementary wrote book reports about him. Old folks at the Royal Manor Alzheimer's Wing recalled that he played a mean fiddle, putting bony finger to withered lip. They thought they'd met him once, perhaps at a barn dance, or maybe it was a barn raising? Regardless, Hollensbee was a hero to almost everyone in Athens. But most heroes aren't simple. Most heroes foster a secret or two, just to keep things interesting.

+++

Athens, Ohio presents herself best in summer. The hardwood forests that surround the city leaf out to a heightened state of green that burns your retinas. There is a constant low vibration, a background cicada hum. If clear and cooler air has crept in from the north, an afternoon in a hammock strung between maples is a grocery-store sample of eternity. Later, at night, you'll stand a good chance of seeing the Milky Way like a gray smear across the black. But if thick and humid air flows in from the south or west, you'll sweat just breathing, even in the shade of the deep front porches that line the quiet streets below the university. You won't sleep well at all, the sheets stuck to your back, and all your creases damp. Heat lightning will pepper the night sky with mute flashes like torches brandished behind clouds. Ceiling fans will rotate in their hopeless trudge. You'll smell ozone in the air—a scent like automobile antifreeze. The unease will build on itself until you hear the first rush of air that flips the maple leaves to their silvery undersides, announcing the storm, and then you'll have about a minute or so to race through the house and close the window sashes before the sky purges its weight of water.

+++

That particular summer, I became one with couch and weather. I'd been laid off on the first of May from my old firm and waiting for something new to shock my defibrillated soul. Kate left on a Sunday, having decided (over the long, charcoal-scented Memorial Day weekend) that she needed to be with someone who kept to an upward trajectory through life. She moved to Indianapolis. Big cities were bound to have a greater concentration of the young and trajectoried.

After that, time slowed around me, except at the mailbox. The bills kept arriving in their usual steady stream, and I stacked them unopened on top of the bookcase, as if they'd eventually tire of my neglect and re-enter the mail stream of their own accord, seeking satisfaction among the deeper-pocketed inhabitants of suburban Cincinnati or Cleveland. I'd started to drift noticeably, having lost both bearing and direction. Up until then, I'd been a mid-level architect—project manager, to be exact—generally responsible for knowing a little something about everything, and always first in line: first to be blamed when things went wrong, and first one let go in a down market. In our office, project managers kept their desks bare, one empty copier-paper box placed close at hand on

Friday afternoons and stowed away again on Monday mornings. One thing they don't teach you in architecture school: you'll need a Plan B sooner or later, as soon as the next recession crests the horizon, so you best think ahead and pick a second career that's somewhat related—sales rep for a plumbing or lighting manufacturer, kitchen make-overs, that sort of thing. Many, by default, end up doing interior renovation. The other thing they don't teach you in architecture school is what a messy second career interior renovation can be; and I don't mean decrepit, debris-strewn farmhouses full of naked copper wiring, or gypsum dust filling your hair and lungs, although there are plenty of those types of annoyances to deal with. I'm talking about the kind of messy that only results from getting tangled up with people bound up in all their own entanglements. Just as with older homes, people never lead to easy solutions, just deepening degrees of complicated.

+++

Early that same spring, the rumor of a possible sale of the Hollensbee place had snaked its way across town. The old mansion had been up for sale intermittently for years, with no takers. Everyone was convinced that an increasingly desperate city administration had fallen into cahoots with some big Columbus developer who wanted the land for student housing, just like they'd done up at Ohio State, and they were all (developers and politicians) just biding their time until the city could enact eminent domain legislation on the property and sentence the weary Federalist-style behemoth to the wrecking ball. But they had one big problem. The Ohio Civil War Trust owned that particular ten acres of land and the 1840s-era structure that sat on it (the main house was that old, not the additions) and they were offering it for the token price of five-thousand dollars, to anyone who would sign a contract promising to renovate the structure and maintain it unaltered for a minimum period of twenty-five years. I tallied my life savings. Nine thousand, four hundred and ten.

I recalled bits of what I'd learned about the mansion in grade school. Its benefactor, Nathaniel Gaines Hollensbee, was alternately painted by local historians as a general-practice physician, confirmed lush, and suspected conductor on the Underground Railroad. Countless scores of runaway slaves, exhausted and hungry and draped in clothing still wet from crossing the Ohio, were said to have taken one last bit of refuge there with Hollensbee before venturing into the vast and foreign and free North.

The Official Town Understatement of Athens, Ohio: the Hollensbee House needed work. What it needed most was a millionaire history buff with an itchy Visa finger, but what it got instead was institutionalized neglect. Due to lack of funds, the non-profit Trust had had no choice but to defer decades of routine maintenance. The roof had been allowed to deteriorate and cave in in several places, which made way for water damage, dark swirls of mold, a filthy squadron of pigeons. Neighborhood kids had broken most of the windows. The ornate plaster moldings under the roof cornice were flaking and falling in chunks. I witnessed these horrors myself, guided by a prim and cedar-scented widow from the Trust. She showed me around and spoke incessantly, as if her words could weave floating curtains to mask the sharp smell of mildew or the sparkling clouds of dust our feet raised in sunlit rooms. She spoke of noble things, like reclaiming history. She lauded Heritage and worshipped Potential. She brightened visibly when I'd told her I was an architect with some time on my hands. "We can save her, can't we?" she asked. I nodded. It was the only kind thing to do.

+++

As soon as the roofing work was done, right after Labor Day, I headed for the cellar. I knew that's where anything really interesting was likely to be found. Three of the walls in the cellar were constructed of massive fieldstone, cut into blocks three feet high by four feet long and set tight together in thin mortar beds. The north wall, however, was formed of much smaller stone, more randomly laid up. I used a hammer to sound the stones. They had the telltale high-pitched retort of a thin wall. Using a crowbar and sledge, I opened a hole in the wall near the base, big enough to crawl through. The next thing I did was call Corinda Baxter.

+++

If you lived in Athens for any length of time, you would have probably gotten to know Corinda Baxter, branch manager of Citizens Savings & Loan. She'd faced two decades of obstacles to get there; being born black and female into the world of small-town conservatives came with a dose of thinly veneered bigotry than most could not survive. Corinda did better than survive. She wore large feathered hats on Sunday mornings and owned four types of parakeets and sang alto in the choir at Cedars of Lebanon Baptist over on Buckeye Street. Her family had roots in Athens deeper than a livestock well. That family told generations of Hollensbee stories to generations of young Baxters. I did my banking at Society, over on Sycamore, so I didn't know her well at all before that night at the Planning Commission. I suppose I could have been better prepared.

My appearance before the Athens Planning Commission made the front page of the local paper. I'd cultivated the support of the mayor, all of council, four out of five commission members (all but Corinda), the Unified Southern Counties Post of the Ohio Civil War Trust, and all the top movers in the business community. By that point, I was all in—every dollar I'd managed to scrape together was already spent, on the purchase price of the property or on the renovation costs, with just enough left for the insurance premium. There was nothing left for contingencies, which is no way to start a reno project.

Corinda was well-connected and forceful and left no confusion in anyone's mind on the topic—she wanted that damn house destroyed. She shouted that Hollensbee was burning in hell, and his house should, too. I suppose no one could blame her, based on the story she'd heard since childhood, told by her in the packed town auditorium with the same full-on fury once used by her great-grandmother, Mama Bernadine Baxter:

Hollensbee was involved in the Underground Railroad, for certain, but his motivations were governed by self-interest. If a fugitive black family could pay, they'd be given safe haven and provisions to continue their journey north. For those that had nothing, there awaited the penalties under the Fugitive Slave Act of 1850. If they didn't have money, but had a fair-looking woman or girl among them, something could usually be arranged, and if things weren't arranged to Hollensbee's liking, the escapees would invariably be ambushed as they left the cellar and returned to their owners in the South, with Hollensbee's pockets fuller for his part. On the night of November the fourteenth, 1859, this was the case. Bounty hunters waited at the gate. They'd been informed that a group of penniless men and older, bent-backed women were leaving for Michigan under cover of darkness. One young slave, a boy named Bartholomew, went outside to piss at the tree line and overheard the hushed drawl of southerners nearby. He hid in the brush, waiting for a chance to run back to the cellar. It never came. The other men and women emerged from the cellar with their few belongings, led by Hollensbee, prepared to travel for days on foot and never expecting to end up shackled and piled into a wagon. It was over within minutes. As the runaways sat, bound and stunned, Bartholomew crept back down to the cellar and hid for an hour, until the mercenaries and their human cargo had started south and Hollensbee came back inside, slamming the front door, his footsteps thumping the floorboards above Bartholomew's head. Hollensbee was furious. His payment had been a fraction of what he'd anticipated, cut by the southerners because they'd counted one less slave than expected, the best one, the youth still in his working prime. Bartholomew knew he had only moments to act. He would surprise Hollensbee as the doctor descended to the cellar. From his hiding place behind the stairs, Bartholomew thrust his arms through the gap between stair treads and grabbed at Hollensbee's ankles. The man tumbled forward to the bottom, hitting his forehead against wood, dropping his gun to the cellar floor. Bartholomew sprang from the shadows and lunged for it, but Hollensbee was closer. The barrel of the weapon wavered between them for long seconds, until Hollensbee's finger found the trigger. Tiny shards of lightning tore through Hollensbee's right leg. The rest shredded the boy, killing him instantly. This was not malice on the part of Hollensbee, just simple precaution. Any knowledge of his ugly business had to die there on the dirt floor as well.

When Corinda finished her speech, the town hall auditorium fell silent. Corinda sat down, trembling. The chair called for a vote. Several Baxters seated in the rear of the auditorium erupted in shouts, calling for my renovation plan to be tabled pending further research of clues regarding the house's history. The Trust folks shouted back. The chairman gaveled them all quiet. I stood and asked to be recognized. I said that I wanted to move forward with the project; that I'd sunk everything into the renovation, and that if it failed, I did, too, and besides that, saving it was the right thing for Athens. I turned to Corinda. I told her that I respected her difference of opinion, but that we should never forget that seventy-one percent of "history" is "story." I offered to have Corinda visit the house during the renovation. Corinda nodded. One of the Baxters applauded. The chair called once again for a vote. My proposal passed, four yeas to one nay.

The most important thing about public meetings is that every word is recorded.

+++

Corinda followed me down to the cellar. I held her hand to steady her as she stepped through the rubble of musty, turned earth and broken stone. I held a flashlight to the hole I'd made. Through the hole, we glimpsed a second wall of larger fieldstone. Protruding from a joint in the stone was a corroded length of chain, and a rusted ring of iron. Threaded through the ring was an ochre length of human femur. Next to the femur, a scattering of other smaller bones, and a skull with its face resting in the dirt, as if sleeping. Among the bones, a leather-bound book and a canvas sack full of coins.

I saw Corinda buckle at the knees. I grabbed her around the waist and started to pull her back from the hole, but she resisted. She reached inside instead, and let the chain slide through her palm.

+++

Here's the conundrum of historical renovation: in order to save an aged piece of architecture, you must first threaten its destruction. You start by getting the historical folks to set its value high, almost priceless, using some sort of government document. Now it's worth a lot, in theory, on paper. You've set its gallows price. So, you insure it for that amount— the amount that the document says it will eventually be worth. Then, right after it is insured, but before much work is done, there comes that awful period of moral weightlessness when, contrary to logic, the damn thing is worth more leveled than upright.

+++

I sat on the front porch with her for a while, with no words. Or maybe it was too many, clogging her throat.

"It's got to come down," Corinda said eventually, staring straight ahead. "It doesn't deserve another day."

I toyed with my flashlight. On. Off.

"This is why things never get better," she said. "We take the past and we scrape at it and paint it pretty and try to forget what it looked like before, what's still there underneath. Blood and ghosts never leave easy. They soak into the cracks and worm themselves behind walls and they aren't going anywhere. Once they're into the bones of a place, the dead just keep eating away at the living."

"What if it becomes a museum?" I asked. "Would that make a difference? Or maybe a bed and breakfast that caters to history buffs? You know, teaching people about what really went on up North during the final days of slavery—that there was equal treachery on both sides of the issue. Maybe fill the place with purpose; some kind of positive energy?"

Corinda shook her head. "It's gone too deep for that. Like when a pasture's overrun by kudzu. You got to burn it out, down to the roots, and start fresh."

"I make a living by building, not wrecking," I said. "I don't know how to do anything else but renovate."

"That's the basic problem with renovation," she said. "If you only fix the things that are easy to get at, then you're just an illusionist. Just another peddler, selling suckers on your rotten fruit. No offense."

"None taken," I said, a mutually agreeable lie. "Are you ready to read it?"

She nodded.

We took turns holding the cracked leather binding in our hands, deciphering the slanted ink that formed the final paragraphs on yellowed pages:

If anyone should find these remains, and this money, and should wonder to whom they belonged, and what transpired in this house that would result in such a curious end as this, with an unfortunate man's burial behind a wall, read on.

The group of escaped slaves which arrived at my door on the night of November the ninth,

1859, numbered thirteen in total and contained among them a most amenable young woman whose skin was not that deepest brown, but lighter, in a shade much like a doe's hide, and she came at night when I called for her and she did the things I asked her to do. Her brother was a member of this same party as well, an enterprising youth. This lad, answering to the name Bartholomew, seemed to me aged beyond his meager years and cunning beyond his station. I admit that I took a liking to him at once. If he knew what transpired between his sister and me, then he did not show it. I must believe that the girl kept her discretion about those matters.

On the third day of preparations for travel north, the lad asked to venture beyond my property, and I said to him that he should not be seen about in daylight, but that if he wanted to hunt game after dusk, for their journey's provisions, he could do so.

On the fourth night after their arrival, the boy left at supper with a weapon of mine and did not return. In truth, I did not expect to see him again.

It was on the fifth night, as the former slaves prepared to depart, that Bartholomew arrived, and with him a group of armed Alabama renegades, some on horseback, others driving a wagon. From my porch, I witnessed the commotion and the random gunfire that followed, and the capture of the runaways. I fled into this house, locked the door, and without thought hid nearby, behind the stairs in the cellar. I listened to the band of criminals batter the front door with their boots and rifle butts until it burst from its frame. It was Bartholomew who found me. I saw the white rings of his eyes in the darkness, wide with danger, staring at me through the dark treads of the stair, and in the light of the lantern he carried I saw him draw a pistol from within his coat, but I already had my gun on him and pulled my trigger before he could.

The boy was bled out by the time I reached him. Much of his gut had disappeared, and what was left could not have been repaired by me, nor by the most skilled of surgeons. I left him there and sat a long while in silence before I could climb the stairs. Later, I would return to seal his body behind an inner wall of stone.

By the time I emerged from the cellar, the southerners and their wagonload of spoils were gone. At the spot of the capture, a small canvas sack of money lay in the dirt. I did not count it, not then or ever. I do not wish to know what price would be placed upon twelve betrayed lives and a thirteenth caught up in its own snare of greed. Whatever amount it is, it is an Abomination, and should never be touched by another man's hands, for it bears the curse of Judas. For now, it must stay with the boy. He can fight Satan for it, on God's Dread Day of Judgment.

Reader, I am not an evil man, but I confess to be a weak man. If survival is a sin, then I am a devout sinner.

God have mercy on my soul.

N. G. H.

Corinda smeared wet streaks wide across her cheeks.

I offered her a cigarette. She waved me off and pulled one of her own from her purse, along with a cheap disposable lighter.

"Do you get it now?" she said, taking a long inhale and flicking the lighter's wheel with her thumb. "Don't you see that it can't remain? Not one more day."

The rumble of a coal train rolled across the town from the east, its hundred-car load of West Virginia lignite headed for a power plant further north. Railroads, a century and a half later, still pulling cargoes north, still pushing money south.

I stood and gathered up my toolbox and water jug. "I'm leaving for the evening," I said.

"Got to pick up some hand-carved crown molding at a salvage yard down in Marietta. Can I trust you here alone?"

Corinda remained on the porch, staring at nothing, lighter in one hand, cigarette dangling from the fingers of the other.

I stopped at the door of my pick-up.

"Make sure you stub that out good," I told her.

+++

Earlier that afternoon, while I waited for Corinda to arrive, I'd wandered the house and gathered the drop cloths into a pile in the center of the drawing room. I collected paint cans, adhesives, cleaning solvents. Hours later, halfway to Marietta, I pulled over at a truck stop diner, ordered a BLT, and dialed the Athens police. I told them about a very uncomfortable conversation I'd had with Corinda Baxter that afternoon, over at the Hollensbee House, and how agitated she seemed, almost mentally unbalanced. As chance would have it, they'd just received the first panicked calls from neighbors who'd noticed flames shooting from the old mansion, blowing out the leaded glass panes from first floor windows, reaching for the roof.

I figured I'd be implicated first, of course, and I was. Sheriff Holtz questioned me first thing the next morning, but I was out the door by ten, quietly exonerated by the combination of alibi, cell phone records, and two diner waitresses, my truck-stop eyewitnesses. The Trust considered suing me but soon thought better of it; I'd left myself a hole by making sure that my list of contractual indemnifications included the phrase "illegal acts of others." Even after so many plans, there would still be some people who thought I'd been paid off by the city, or a developer, or both, which is why I needed Corinda. The truth, even if someone cared enough to uncover it, would have been swallowed up in seconds by the deep-rooted prejudices and the newer, sexier fictions. This is exactly what I meant at the beginning, about people and messiness. I'd managed to pull it off, yet somehow, I couldn't eat. My insides blistered with acid. I waited weeks for the insurance check. I feigned despondency. I walked the sleepy residential streets of Athens in darkness until the traffic lights downtown cycled to off-hours mode, a constant blinking red. I liked Corinda Baxter, and I took no pleasure in watching her life derail, but the absence of malice didn't figure into my decision at all. It was simply an abundance of precaution, I kept telling myself, a protection of my investment. It was me keeping the tarps tied down.

+++

One last thing I've learned from years spent doing renovations: on clear spring or autumn nights, like the ones back in Ohio, when the temperature drops fast, an old house's materials contract and that's when it chooses to speak out, in creaks of floor beams and groans of rafters. I've been known to sit cross-legged in the darkened rooms of my renovations and just listen, sometimes for an hour or more, to the pops and the cracks. Cool air rushes through, attic to foyer, and you almost swear they're breathing. I never bothered to listen on that first job, however. Not at the Hollensbee house. Some old places are just too far gone, and best sacrificed to save the young. Those are the houses that you can't have talking to anyone.

Pancho

One fork in the path, two choices—the right one and I'm back at camp before dark; the wrong one would take me out to Interstate 77 or the mud-colored Muskingum River before I realized I was lost, certainly for the night, maybe for two. I was used to getting left behind, though. I'd learned to read dirt.

The lights were on over the cabin porches by the time I got back.

Kevin looked up as I slammed the screen door. "Your horse sucks, dickhead!" he laughed. "Joey, you got the worst horse in camp!" Robbie gave me the finger. The fat kid, Edwin, called me a loser again. Loser Joey and his loser horse. When names had some whiff of truth to them, they seemed to cut meaner, like dull blades, their edges rubbed in salt. My truth: I didn't like what I saw in the mirror in 1977. I was wire-thin, had these protruding ears, big plastic-rimmed eyeglasses. When Frank assigned horses to the Cheyenne campers, he sized me up, pointed to a sad-looking chestnut gelding and said, "Pancho."

Pancho hated movement. He liked standing still, dazed, chewing greenery. He didn't want a rider, or to ride. Resistance was his only weapon. Other kids' horses had energy. Robbie couldn't keep his filly Duchess from randomly busting out into trots or flat-out sprints. If Pancho had ever had that kind of spirit, something had killed it off. If Bear Creek were long ago, in Nevada, someone would have already put a bullet between Pancho's eyes and called it progress.

Spending two weeks of summer at Bear Creek Dude Ranch was supposed to get us away from the names. Mom was busy all spring talking to lawyers and chain-smoking again and crying on the back porch after chasing us into bed. Dad was three months into the twelve-month stay he owed the State of Ohio for embezzlement. As Dad explained it, he had borrowed some money, but those damn bastards hadn't given him the chance to pay it back. Then he was carted off to Youngstown. We saw him two Sundays a month. I was twelve, and this was the world I got, ill-fitted and cheaply sewn.

Mom wanted us out of the house, me and Kevin. Kevin was "acting out," she said. Fist-fighting, shoplifting, calling her a bitch. She wanted us to grow up into better men. We needed better role models. We needed summer camp. We needed to be around horses, and to be around the kind of men who were around horses.

We were both placed in Cheyenne Cabin. Our counselor was Frank. Frank was twenty-two and looked three-parts biker, one-part cowboy. He had hair down to his shoulder blades. He listened to AC/DC and kept a pack of Marlboros stuffed up under the sleeves of his T-shirts, like an extra squared-off muscle on top of all the other rounder ones. Frank smoked weed after lights-out (said Kevin). Frank was having sex with some of the female counselors (reported Kevin, he'd seen it). I was scared of Frank, because I wanted to know more about him, and because Kevin wanted to be him.

About half an hour after lights out, I heard Kevin climb down from his bunk and slip out the front door. I waited twenty minutes.

Between the camp light poles and the half-moon, I could make out the trail to the counselors' cabins. There were lights on in the first one. I circled it, looking for Kevin, peering into windows. No Kevin.

I found a folding chair to stand on. In the first window: pizza boxes, beer cans. The second: Tammy the aquatics instructor was straddling

Alex, counselor from Apache. Tammy's bra was off and Alex cradled a round breast in each hand.

The third window was the back bedroom. I could stand on the edge of the rain barrel and just see into the corner of the glass. A lamp was on. Frank was there, holding a Polaroid. Every few seconds a bright flash blinded me. Kevin stood across from him, drinking a beer. Kevin's shorts were pulled down to his knees.

I felt like puking. My foot slipped. I fell off the barrel into a holly bush, banging my knees against the cedar siding on the way down. I wasn't fast enough. Frank had a flashlight on me before I could slip into the shadows.

I was late to the stables the next morning for the trail ride. I still felt sick.

I went to gear up Pancho, but he wasn't in his stable. In his place stood a big gray Appaloosa, muscles revving and rippling, a good two feet taller than Pancho.

Frank shuffled past. "You're on Ranger now," he said, studying his clipboard.

Days later, back at home, Mom asked how camp was. I said "fine." It was the only possible answer. There was no way to explain how I liked the fizz of cold beer on my tongue, how it felt to be cool for once, how I didn't mind the flash in my eyes as long as no one touched.

Small Engine Repair

When I was nineteen and twenty, I worked summers at one of those garden center places in Seven Hills, a suburb south of Cleveland. It was modest pay in return for being outdoors, watering flats of petunias, hefting bags of mulch into trunks, farmer-tanning, flirting with the cashier girls in their halter tops and short-shorts. It was modest pay in return for the clandestine drinking of Rolling Rock from emerald-green cans kept chilly in a buried cooler, its lid camouflaged with clumps of dried grass hidden between the tarp-covered greenhouse frames.

A rehabbing burnout named Dale fixed small engines out of a rented shop located in the basement of the main barn. The old man who owned the whole place tolerated Dale because he paid his rent. The old man saved his hate for the small flock of urban pigeons that was trying to colonize the property, so he had no problem with Dale's air rifle going off at closing time.

I had nothing in common with Dale. He'd flunked out of regular high school but stumbled upon vocational school; found small engine repair like some people find Jesus. Found it understandable. Gas mixes with air and explodes in a controlled chamber. Gas tank, gas filter, air filter, carburetor. Starter cord and a spark plug to provide the ignition. Oil chamber to lubricate the parts, drain plug, a transmission that turns piston action into blade rotation. Dale was confident in this knowledge, which put him slightly ahead of me. To Dale, I was a college boy who didn't deserve what he had, and had no clue what he didn't. Translated to gun-speak, the most I'd ever done was plink tin cans at Boy Scout camp, years ago. Dale, however, could take out pigeons with a single shot.

One evening, Dale hands me his Browning .22. "Get that one over there," he says. He points to a white pigeon with gray wings, pecking in the grit on the asphalt driveway. I take aim, I shoot. The pigeon jerks sideways and tries to fly, but flops back down on one side. It stands back up, tries again, flops again. Its left wing drags on the ground, useless. It is now a pedestrian. I'm nauseous with the bird's flailing.

"Let me have another shot," I say. To end the misery.

"No way," Dale answers. "Only one shot, College."

Dale would never let me touch the Browning again. He wouldn't shoot the walker himself either. He'd just laugh and point to it stumbling around and say, "Hey, hey College, there's your little buddy over there!" Once in a while, I'd leave a fistful of grass seed for the white pigeon, and when Dale caught me doing it he called me a pussy.

The following summer, I moved on. I joined the Teamsters and got a better-paying job driving forklifts and loading fifty-three-foot semi-trailers at the Seaway Foods warehouse in Bedford Heights. There, I befriended a bunch of the old-timers, the senior operators who trained me. One guy, an aging black man named Terrence, stocky and quiet, cornered me in the break room one day.

"You going to college?" he asked.

"Yup, one more year left," I said.

Terrence stared at me with an expression that could bend spoons. "If I see you back here next summer," he said, "I will personally kick your skinny white ass." Not a threat, I realized, but friendly advice. Keep moving ahead, son. No rest, no rust. No returning. A modern urban take on "Go west, young man"—the long-favorite saying of those who wouldn't go, couldn't go themselves.

Years later, on a whim, I climbed into my car and drove past the old garden center, but it was out of business; the old man had sold the property to the car dealership next door and moved to a beachfront condo in Naples. The rows of red geraniums had been replaced by rows of red Chevy Cavaliers. I pulled over and wondered what became of Dale. Was there a Terrence for him, someone to tell him that the garden center shutting down wasn't a bad thing; that it could actually be the best thing that ever happened to him? I'll never know, but I'm a writer, so I craft an ending that suits me: he never gateway'd into heroin. He didn't max out his life in a tiny, rented mower shop. I want to believe that if he had it to do all over again, he would have let me keep the Browning another ten seconds and I would have made things right.

Mr. Forecloser

There's been another victim, another family gone, this time over in Ohio City, and the usual three days pass before Mr. Forecloser's cell phone rings. It's Martha at Third Federal, one of his best customers. He cuts his lunch short, drives west on the Shoreway and rolls to a stop along the fractured curb in front of the scene. He pulls on his Carhartt jacket, feels for his knife, pushes open the front door.

They left in a hurry. There are some women's clothes still hanging in closets, Jay-Z posters left on a bedroom ceiling. The gangbangers have already come and gone—there's a Goony Boyz tag sprayed across the entire living room wall, some F-bombs, the C-word, but luckily not much in the way of wall damage. He finds the basement stairs and runs a quick check, for druggies and homeless. The scrappers haven't raped the copper plumbing yet. He makes the calls to cancel the utilities.

Then he starts his window count.

Mr. Forecloser wears a tool belt, the kind with a pouch for everything: screws, cordless driver, nails, hammer—tools for treating symptom, not disease. There's nothing he could carry that could really do any good against this particular breed of evil anyway. Nothing that could neutralize, say, foreign outsourcing, derivative trading.

He drives an old stake-bed truck held together with Bondo and fingercrossings. The truck carries his stack of five-eighths plywood, and his toolbox full of hasps and padlocks, and his paints. He needs to get the truck fixed, but the money for the repairs is the money he uses for paint. The paint is for the plywood; the plywood for the windows. He can't expense the cost of the paint. What's wrong with bare plywood? his clients asked. They never understood, so he tried explaining it to his wife. She listened. Then she said, So what's wrong with bare plywood?

He's painted hundreds of billowing curtain scenes, kids' faces peering out, cats curled up on sunny sills, red geraniums in pots. He tries for photo-realistic shadowing, and he's not afraid of bold colors. He thinks he's good with faces, not so much with hands, so his scene-people always have their hands hidden. Hands are tough, even Rembrandt said so. He'd like to get better at hands, so maybe one of these days a little kid of his might wave hello from a bedroom window.

Mr. Forecloser used to be an artist, locally known, back when the economy tolerated artists. He held exhibitions at respectable galleries downtown, and Wealthy Collectors carried checkbooks while they discussed his work, and Middle-Class Admirers sipped drinks and talked as if they probably would have bought one, if only they had remembered to bring their checkbooks.

When it all collapsed, he almost lost his own place. His wife shoved the phone into his hand. He called his Wealthy Collectors and left awkward, stammering messages until one called back. One collector in Shaker Heights knew a guy, a senior asset manager at a big mortgage lender. The lender guy was swamped with vacant properties. Do you have a pen handy? By the way, the collector asked, where can I see your current work? Mr. Forecloser didn't answer, but said thanks, hung up.

What's funny is that just a few miles from Shaker Heights, over in Glenville, you can see whole streets full of his work. On sunny days, between runs, Mr. Forecloser parks his truck on a dead-end street and closes his eyes and concentrates until he can almost hear lawnmowers and playground-laughs and dog-barks, tries to forget that life here has become exactly five-eighths of an inch thick, tries to forget that his whole city is bleeding out, one four-by-eight sheet at a time, and he's the tardy paramedic with the rainbow Band-Aids. He opens his eyes, sees the static, painted faces of the children in the bedroom windows.

Wave! he shouts. You little bastards, wave! Like the living should. Like the leaving should.

Brothers of the Salvageable Crust

Professor Leonard Littmann had just announced Interaction Node 42. With a flick of a switch, the house lights came up in the main auditorium of Townsend Hall. Littmann—middle-aged, adjunct, embarrassingly unpublished—smiled as he scanned the rows of the young women filling the seats. His bed-tanned hands gripped the podium like an unwilling dance partner.

"Consider the conundrum: When is silence louder than communication? When does communication become just a quieter form of silence? My dear ladies, can you see where this confrontation is headed?" asked Littman, pulling at the sleeves of the salmon-colored cardigan tied over his shoulders. "What would you establish as an appropriate response/non-response ratio for Dave as he attempts to face this rather significant setback?"

Dave, whose real name was Rusty, shifted uncomfortably in his steel-toes. The heat thrown down by the spotlights was broiling him in his flannel shirt, frying his bald spot. Littman had never told him anything about any damn spotlights or Interaction Nodes, let alone a theater full of coeds dissecting his every move. But shame on me, Rusty thought, he hadn't asked what to expect when he signed on to play Dave Dithers in Littmann's grad-level course, Sociology 551: Interactive Marriage Simulation, or something like that; he wasn't quite sure of the words, but it was high-level stuff, certainly a bit beyond him. Darlene Dithers, Dave's difficult and sporadically attractive faux wife, was portrayed by Melanie Grabowski, who was supplementing the income from her other part-time job at Food Services. At that particular moment, Melanie had her head in her hands on the opposite side of their prop kitchen table. She'd just finished delivering the session's agitated Darlene monologue: "Dave (something something) all the empathy of a pipe wrench (something something) emotionally bankrupt and I'm not sure we can even go on from here." Someone in Row G applauded a little. Melanie pounded the Formica tabletop for good measure.

The day's Core Relationship Stressor, or CRS, was part one of a two-session focus on Emotional Unavailability. Previous weeks had been a parade of such manufactured crises as Sudden-Onset Unemployment, Infidelity, the Fertility Clinic Follies, a special double session on Rebellious Drug-Peddling Offspring /School Expulsion right before midterms; then after the break came Sexual Dysfunction, Internet Porn Addiction, Parasitic In-Laws, and Adventures in Personal Bankruptcy. He and Melanie were two people who had been through hell together and still had yet to go on a real date, courtesy of Littmann's vision. Each semester, Littmann re-staged his particular brand of social theater, and the sororities supplied one coed to help him stem his loneliness in return for advance copies of final essay questions. The designated Littslut bartered them to the rest of the sorority girls (making up eighty-percent of the class), who in turn bartered them to the field hockey players, who made up ten-percent of the class, who sold them outright to the remaining ten-percent composed of various Not-It-Girl subcastes in cash-only transactions. "Clicks for Chicks" had been the number-one most popular humanities elective at Farmingham College for five years running. It was part institution, part ecosystem. It had its own food chain.

Rusty awaited his cue. Littmann said, "Let's define the choice at this node—does Dave try to emotionally connect with Darlene, or does he walk away? Ready your devices. And…interact."

Rusty considered his instincts, followed by the usual distrust of his instincts. He had already fled backstage when the Results Monitor flashed 74% Try to Connect.

+++

In the tiny locker area behind the stage, Melanie pulled off the frumpy Darlene housecoat and put on her Food Services jacket, which smelled of pilaf and pine cleaner.

"Have any plans later?" Melanie asked, replacing fuzzy slippers with brown flats.

"Got some mowing to finish before it gets dark," Rusty said, and then wanted to say he was free after that, but he debated that last part with himself a little too long. With a half-wave, Melanie left.

Locker time was what Rusty breathed for, those precious few minutes of transition between Melanie the Stranger and Darlene the Fake Spouse. In the warped little solar system that was Farmingham College, even a misshapen asteroid like him found a few moments of perihelion with objects like Melanie; and when the moments came, he gravitated. Melanie had told Rusty about the solid four years she'd put in at her desk in the catacombs below South Dining Hall, and how she'd already been promoted three times, placed on the fast-track, reaching the level of Deputy Starches Coordinator a whole year early. She was the one in charge of menu logistics for breads, yeasted bread-like baked goods, non-yeasted baked goods (including the whole subcategory of cookies and flatbreads), assorted rices, grains, cereals, and every other week, potato products. She shared potatoes in a mediated agreement with Ingrid Holmgren, the pompous bitch in Fresh Produce who filed a union grievance claiming jurisdiction over tubers. Ingrid's lame argument: that most other tubers, like carrots and beets, are actually starchy vegetables, not vegetable-ish starches.

And that was always the problem, wasn't it? All the Ingrids and Littmanns and Marty O'Mearas of the world that were just two-legged delivery systems for a slow poison designed to strangle the dreams out of guys like him. God, the places he could have gone without them! He pictured a cabin big enough for two in Canada somewhere, perched on the edge of a pine forest, and next to it, a large sunny field, and Rusty's half of the field was a 50/50 blend of Kentucky Bluegrass and Red Fescue, neatly mowed in concentric rings, and Melanie's half would be planted in wheat and corn and more types of tubers than that bitch Ingrid Holmgren could ever dream of.

The typical indicators pointed to Melanie pushing thirty, Polish-built, intermittently brunette. And that was just how she described herself, in qualifiers, always in pairs of words like leisurely athletic and Sundayishly Catholic. She tended to let things slip about herself as they sat in front of their lockers and dressed in their Dave and Darlene garb, and when she did, Rusty stopped to feel the magnets banging around inside his gut again, because this was the time for her personal things, heavy and intimate things, shavings from her iron core, like how she pictured her life as a sort of sad rosary—identical concretions of miserable days strung together with a repeating sequence of bad haircuts. Or how no one had ever bought her flowers just for the hell of it. Or how she hasn't had the time for a man, being the only child and thus default caretaker of an obsessive-compulsive hypochondriac mother who insisted on harboring imaginary afflictions in groups of three. Mother Grabowski's current line-up combined a layer of caffeine-induced sleepwalking over a long-suspected urinary tract infection and undiagnosed vertigo. Melanie had been setting her alarm for three in the morning and searching the closets until she found the one Mother G had fallen over and pissed herself in.

Rusty considered square footage once again as he maneuvered the mower deck around the sugar maple saplings next to the Fine Arts building. Success, to him, came in square feet, at least that's how he was raised to think, so he'd been saving up for a place to call his own that would be big enough for someone else to call her own. Again, he added together how much he'd need for himself, how much additional for another, say maybe a Melanie-sized another, and how much more for an another's mother. Could he even afford that much? Maybe so, if that another didn't have a lot of junk, and sometimes brought home Tupperware of excess starches from the dining hall, and if the another's mother was bed-ridden by that time, and pretty much stayed put in a two-foot by six-foot area, well then just maybe. When he got that place of his— when, not if—then he could land his catch, not just drag a bare hook through water like he'd been doing. Rusty told his boss, Marty O'Meara, all three-hundred pounds of Marty, that he was almost ready to move out of the maintenance loft and rent an apartment over in Collegetown, but Marty said yeah, sure Rusty, you'll get a place when I get a treadmill. Marty didn't even own a pair of sneakers.

Rusty shut down the mower deck and fired up the weed-whacker by rote, the same way he sleep-worked and cot-slept and saved his money and avoided temptation as the seasons cycled from plow to mulch to mow to rake. It was the rhythm of the last ten of his thirty years spent keeping up the grounds of The Farmingham College of Liberal Arts. His small set-up in the loft of the Maintenance Building cost him nothing—free cot, free sink and toilet—as long as he agreed to monitor the automated irrigation system after-hours in the summer, and keep the main walks cleared during pre-dawn winter snows. He had a Rec Center pass for showers and his employee discount at the dining hall. He had a couple of co-workers that some might classify as friends, or at least comrades; fellow bare-hook-draggers.

How many times had he and the other grounds crew guys gotten cleaned up at the Rec Center and splashed on some Old Spice and made Ramon promise (in Spanish) to shut his Mexican yap and then went out cruising the chain restaurants up and down the strip, all those Ladies' Nights at Applebee's, but the women in college towns like this were always journal-published or tenure-tracked or research-granted, and when it was their turn to ask him what he did for a living, Rusty mumbled something about horticultural engineering and pretended to feel the vibrations of an incoming call in his front pants pocket, from the deck of cards he pretended was a cell phone, and he said sorry, that's got to be the Smithsonian again, their Civil War rhododendron collection is on life support, and since when am I the only goddamn board-certified stem graft surgeon east of the Mississippi, and ran out the emergency exit.

Rusty drove the equipment back to the Maintenance Building just as the sprinkler heads on the main quad awoke for nocturnal irrigation. Up in his loft, Rusty grabbed a Dr. Pepper from the mini-fridge and stretched out on his cot. He told himself again that he'd have a real bed soon, the kind with a headboard and all, but believed it a little less than he said it, because he still heard little voices sometimes, tiny airline-bottle-sized ones, tink-tinking as they rolled around the vehicle bay, usually right about now, at dusk, just as the neon bar signs downtown flickered and hummed to life, whispering Rusty, you won, you showed us who's boss, now use that self-control, show us how you can stop yourself after just one.

Rusty tried to sleep, but thought about Melanie instead, for hours, still awake when she was probably awakening. He pictured her in flannel, shining a flashlight, eyes dampened, closet after closet.

+++

May 10th was the last day of Littmann's course, and the first day Rusty knew what he needed to do. He hadn't studied his lines. Fifteen minutes into the simulation, he had missed every cue.

Littmann, exasperated, called Interaction Node 63. "Okay, so ladies, Dave's childish little snit here: helpful or not? I'm sensing a big 'not.' In a true partnership, a Synergetic Symbiosis, to use my trademark-pending phrase, I would hope that the Dave would take his passive-aggressive hostility and channel it toward some honest, rewarding interplay with the Darlene, instead of gumming up the relationship gears with his sludge of negativity. But you need to make up your own minds. Ready devices."

The handhelds appeared in a white rash across the auditorium.

"Interact."

Keypads clattered like hailstones.

After ten seconds, the Results Monitor indicated 89% Not Helpful.

"Excuse me, but I'd like to call a Node too," said Rusty.

"You what?" said Littmann.

"I want to call a Node," repeated Rusty.

"You can't call a Node. We just had a Node. And besides, I call the Nodes. And one more thing, you've now received a Not-Helpful for the day, so you're in no position to be pushing the limits, Dave."

"But why can't I call one?"

"Because I am conducting the simulation, DAVE, that's why. An actor can't step out of the simulation, DAVE, that's also why; for to do so would inject inappropriate perspective into the situation. May I remind you, DAVE, that the key to my realistic Interactive Marriage Simulation methodology is, as I will rather eloquently state in my upcoming white paper, the limitation of actors' outside perspectives to only those that real people would experience at that moment. The perspective belongs only to them," gesturing toward the seats. "Years from now, when these students, whom I have the distinct privilege to instruct, find themselves in similar circumstances to the ones you both are rather painfully attempting to portray, they will remember— fondly, I think—their IMS experiences and be able to step back from their marital crises and assess their behavioral options with some degree of perspective."

"I thought you just said that realistic simulations cannot involve perspective," mumbled Rusty.

"Of course, I did!" shouted Littmann, banging the podium with his fist.

"So, we need to keep perspective out of these realistic simulated problems so that someday they," pointing outward, "will be able to put perspective into realistic real problems?"

Littmann's face went momentarily blank.

"I'd like to request interaction on the possibility of Dave extending one Token of Endearment to Darlene right now," Rusty continued.

Littmann choked out his words. "No, absolutely not. No way. You're completely off script, Dave. You are supposed to be Emotionally Unavailable this week, remember? A Token of Endearment, this week? Are you kidding me? Do you enjoy being our human speedbump, Dave? Where was your Token of Endearment three months ago, during Infidelity, when your little supply room rendezvous with…what was her name…"

"Brandy," yelled out one of the sorority girls, the one named Brandy, who got to play Brandy.

"Right, when your little supply room rendezvous with Brandy over there just about doomed your simulated marriage to the simulated crapper? Huh, Dave? What's that? Did you say something? You can't expend a Token, Dave. I believe your emotional account is overdrawn."

Murmurs of approval rose from the dimmed rows of seats. The sorority girls were giving Littmann little mock fist-bumps.

"I'm serious," said Rusty. "I want an answer. Why can't Dave be there for Darlene right now?"

Melanie looked ill.

Littmann fumed. "Interaction Node 64," he stammered.

Rusty approached the podium, fists balling. "Now you wait just a damn minute..."

"Interaction Node 64!" Littmann cried out, louder, positioning the podium between himself and Rusty. "Consider the conundrum: our Dave, in a grievously misguided effort to focus your empathy on our Darlene, has succeeded instead in drawing your focus to his own antics instead of the CRS, the Core Relationship Stressor. It's a classic misdirection-objection. Okay then, Dave, what if I turn the tables on you a bit? You think what you're doing is right, and yet the scene isn't working—look at Melanie over there, she's absolutely sick. So, if something's wrong, and it's not you, it must be her. Ladies, your choice—do we replace our Dave with someone who is more, shall we say, minimally cooperative, or do we accept and attempt to work through the issue raised by our currently obstructivist Dave, and follow his recommendation to replace Darlene in time for the final exam?"

"Hey, I never suggested replacing Melanie, I mean Darlene," said Rusty.

Littmann ignored him. "It's a simple choice. I would not be forthright with you ladies, however, if I didn't warn you that the effort involved in rehabilitating our current Dave would involve some degree of additional evening workshops and study groups, and we'd have to postpone the final. But that, of course, is your prerogative. Ready devices. Interact."

Rusty looked at Melanie. Melanie stared at her fuzzy slippers until the clicking subsided.

96% Replace Melanie.

Rusty was numb, but still breathing. He was at the bottom of a well, paralyzed, glued to a cot, surrounded by echoes of dripping water. It was the sound of a leaking life, its years draining away, its hopes dissolving. Without her acting gig, Melanie wouldn't be able to afford her mother's care, would never speak to him again, would start the gears turning that would lead straight to him spending the remainder of his years lofted and cotted and alone. A black hole yawned open beneath him, swirling and swallowing everything, but then there came a thin voice like a rope to grab onto, a man's voice, miles away, a far-off Littmannish voice thanking everyone for a rousing end to this semester's simulations. Distant applause spilled over the edge of the hole and rained down on him from above, from the auditorium full of women, and he clawed up the walls and followed it back to its source.

"...and it's been my distinct pleasure to guide you young ladies through this semester's exploration of the complexities that muddle even the most rudimentary specimens of the male species, and the resulting impediments to healthy relationships that are bound to ensue. Dave, or shall I say Rusty—I guess I can go back to calling you that now—I am duly impressed at the push-back during today's class. Quite stimulating, actually, for a final session. I wasn't sure you had it in you. You took it right down to the wire, but with that last-minute outburst of emotional maturity, you've nonetheless proven my hypothesis—that with weeks of helpful interaction on our part, the self-inflicted wounding instincts of an inferior male can be altered to allow the formation of strong and lasting relationships. Ladies, excuse me, but before you leave, I'd be remiss if I didn't take a quick moment to thank my graduate assistant, Elizabeth Duffy, for pulling off the doubly difficult assignment of portraying Melanie Grabowski portraying Darlene Dithers. Simulation within simulation! Well done, my dear. Do you ever wake up and forget your real name?"

Amid laughter and applause, students stood, gathered their things and filed up the aisles and out the rear doors of the auditorium. Elizabeth, acknowledging no one, disappeared into the locker room.

Rusty sat on the edge of the stage, nauseous and adrift. Littmann joined him. They were alone.

"Rusty, this isn't going to help right now, but I had my reasons. If I had told you that you were participating in a course called Inadequate Male Studies, you would have altered your natural instincts, right? Practiced up for the role? Artificially adjusted your actions, out of pride, to better fit some sort of macho stereotype? No, I couldn't have that. I'm a man of science, Rusty. I believe in the scientific method. This is going to be studied and published and then picked apart by my naysayers, so I can't screw this thing up. This had to be a blind study, and the whole marriage simulation thing seemed like a reasonable placebo. You look stunned, Rusty. I'm sorry, I really am, but honestly, didn't you ever ask yourself why the class was comprised entirely of women? Didn't you check the course catalog? Didn't think to do that, right? I guess that's to be expected, that sweet naivete. You'll come to understand, after the initial shock wears off, that my duplicity was necessary. I believe we'll even laugh about this someday. I'll see you and your riding mower out on the quad and I'll wave you down and you'll give me the finger and we'll just laugh. I'll say, 'Hi Rusty' and you'll say, 'Nope, the name's Dave' and we'll chuckle some more and I'll say, 'How about signing up for another simulation?' and you'll say, 'Simulate this, Littmann,' and flip me off again. Ha ha!" coughed Littmann, stunted, as if doling out comfort in a Dixie cup, a grocery-store sample of some future camaraderie.

Rusty could only manage a word. Why.

Littmann put an arm over Rusty's shoulder. "Look, Rusty—imagine the entire male species as one big cherry pie. There are a lot of juicy bites in the center that everyone wants, or else wants to be, and then out on the periphery there's the crust, the part that most people leave on their plates when they've eaten all the good stuff. But we need the crust, don't you see, it's so necessary, because what's a pie without crust? A big sloppy mess of delicious fruit filling, that's what! We need guys like you, Rusty, because you give shape to the rest of us. You show us what we are by showing us what we're not. But there's usually too much crust, isn't there? These big awkward hunks of dough, burnt on the edges— way more than what's needed to hold the thing together. So, my career-defining brainstorm is this: what if I could take a bit of this crust and adopt it as a human renovation project, and get women to add their input throughout the process, and in the end transform some of that crust into more yummy pie-guts, which is what everyone really desires? This is the essence of my work— roaming the back alleys of masculinity and repatriating some of the most tattered and faltering fringe-dwellers of our species. I'm the anti-Darwin, Rusty, and you are my biggest success. I think you might even be ready to find a woman. You've spent your last day as crust, my friend. Let me be the first to welcome you to your new life." And with that, Littmann reached out his other arm and engulfed Rusty in a bearhug.

Rusty's arms hung limp at his side. He swallowed hard. Littmann released. Rusty felt his feet touch the floor, start to lurch toward the exit, but something made him stop and turn, something new, or newly rediscovered, and the final and most indelible image Rusty took with him from all his years at Farmingham was the white flash of Littman's grin gone red from a collision with his fist.

+++

Three hours later, Rusty slumped across the rear seat of a Greyhound bus. He had had forty dollars cash left in his pocket when he stumbled out of Ricky's Midtown Tavern, so he was headed somewhere that was exactly forty dollars away; maybe not enough to escape Ohio, but then again, the destination wasn't important, as long as rents were affordable and there were lawns that needed mowing and it was miles and miles from Melanie, from Littmann, from Farmingham; miles from the backstage dressing room where Ed the Janitor happened to be cleaning out the remaining contents of Rusty's locker. Ed delivered a grass-stained sweatshirt to the lost and found box in the front lobby of Townsend Hall, and the Rentals section of the Farmingham Sentinel to the trash. The only other item left in the locker, on the top shelf, was a cheap glass vase full of pink and white carnations. There was no note attached. Ed the Janitor shrugged. He decided he'd take the arrangement home and give it to his wife, who had just been saying the other day that she couldn't understand how she had ended up with exactly the kind of guy she never thought she would, the kind that would never bring a woman flowers just for the hell of it. I thought you got some kind of training, she had said. What the hell is your problem, Ed? Didn't that guy Littmann teach you anything?

What We Were When We Drew What We Drew

I think Gabe must have been about fourteen when he lost his face, right before Christmas, body pinned in the back seat of the accordioned sedan, the flames reaching him just before the jaws of life did.

Gabe lived in the hospital for half a year, then all of sudden he showed up at school at the end of August with his head looking like it had been dipped in melted wax. He could still see through one eye, through a pseudo-eye like a hotel peephole poked into the scar tissue when it was still wet. He breathed through two holes in the middle, heard through two fleshy seashells for ears, ate through a dry crack in the plaster of his thickened skin. They say that this skin came from somewhere else on him—a second wave of unsettling imagery.

The teachers did their best to protect him, but it was inevitable; in the class-change scrums, in the locker-room corners, kids pinned him up against walls and graffitied his blank face with Sharpies. Smiley faces, jack-o'-lanterns every October and hearts at Valentine's, swear words, doodles of vaginas and penises, middle finger salutes. Gabe didn't cry—or if he did, we couldn't tell, his tear ducts welded shut by the heat—he just scrubbed his face clean after every incident, after the bell rang, after they moved on to some other victim. Sometimes kids drew on him as a novelty, like trying a joint, but Gabe had his regulars, too. I tried not to be one of them.

Twenty years later, just when I've almost forgotten him, here he is at University Hospital's fundraiser for their new Pediatric Burn Unit. A poster sits on a gold stand in the lobby: Author Gabriel Rutledge Book Signing Tonight! Salon B.

I wait in line. There are stacks of hardcovers near him. His memoir, *Facing Faceless*, is a best seller—feel-good book of the year, darling of book clubs coast to coast. Women's cheeks are wet when they walk past me clutching their signed copies tight to their chests.

I almost leave a few times, my needle swinging between speak now and forever hold, but suddenly it's high school again and there is nothing between me and that waxy visage of his.

"Hey Gabe," I manage. "It's Steve Geddis. Remember me? From high school. Stevie, from Glenhaven Drive?"

"Yeah," he says. "Right. Steve Geddis. So how are you?"

"Good," I say. "Real good. Hey, congrats on your book! Congrats on, um, everything."

"Thanks," he says.

The lighting casts a gloss on the scar tissue like a screen and I flip back through all the things I ever saw there.

"Hey, I'm sorry," I stammer.

He doesn't respond.

"I want to say I'm sorry for what they did to you back then, in school. What I did to you. It wasn't right. You didn't deserve it."

"It's okay," he says. "It was never about me, Steve. You know that."

"Still," I say. "Just…not right."

He leans toward me, his voice lower. "You know how I survived high school? I learned that my blank face, this emptiness, was kind of like a mirror to people. Whatever they wrote on me was really written about them. The ones that wrote the ugliest things, I could picture those kids later at home, being beaten by dads or step-dads, ignored by drunk moms. Kids who tried slitting wrists, swallowing handfuls of pills."

My mind races, recalling what I'd drawn, and how I could have.

"Let me ask you a question," he says. "Do you like yourself yet, Steve?"

I feel the eyes of everyone in line scorching holes in my back.

"Would it help you to write on me one more time, then erase it? Or write something new? What do you need from me?" He pushes a Sharpie toward me.

"No," I say, "just, maybe if you could just sign a copy for me. That'd be great."

He grabs the Sharpie back, opens the front cover of a nearby copy, fingers past four pages and carefully writes on the title page. He closes it and slides it over to me.

"Thanks for coming out," he says.

In the car, I turn on the map light. On the title page, between my name and his, he's drawn a head, and where the face should be, there's a picture of dick, with a big X through it. Except for the X, it's exactly as I remember.

Assisted Living

Lily had written these letters on the back of her hand, in red ink: G. A. L. S. It was an example of something, another word she couldn't recall, but the missing word meant that all the letters stood for other words, a sequence of four words she must remember, because the words stood for actions and it was the actions that were important. She took a breath, trapped it. Her fingers twitched. She mouthed G. G was for Grasp. Grasp something. Grasp. A. A. Her vision clouded. Her concentration faded, fragmented into static. A. A was what?

Marcus stood nearby, watching. She wished he would say something, but he never did. Not until later. He always wrote on a clipboard first, talked later, in private.

A was what? Arms? Maybe Arms? She leaned forward and took the two small hands in her own.

L. L was for Lift. That she remembered. Lift. Strong but gentle, was what Marcus taught. Strong but gentle.

She pulled on the tiny arms, careful not to jerk, but applied steady force. The baby's torso rose up off the table, and the head followed, at first, until without warning, it flopped backwards, heavy, a water balloon, a dainty sand bag. Lily screamed and let go of the baby, to try to cushion the head from hitting the tabletop. Lily's arms flailed, shot everywhere like live wires. The baby lolled to one side, fell off the edge of the table, hit the linoleum floor. Its rubber head bounced just once.

Lily, hysterical, fell to her knees and patted at the air around the doll, trying to comfort it, afraid to touch it. Marcus slid his arms under her shoulders and helped Lily to her feet. Lily sobbed into his chest.

Sorry, she said, sorry. I screwed up. Broken broken egg.

It's all right, said Marcus. You can do this, Lily. You've still got a few months to practice. You and Robert can do this. Remember: Grasp Ankles, Lift, Scoop. GALS. Start by lifting the legs. When you scoop, you start under the baby's butt and slide up the back, palm up, and your palm stops underneath the back of the baby's head. That way, the head is always protected. Babies have weak necks and delicate heads, right?

Like eggs, said Lily, choking on mucus. Shells and yolks.

Just like eggs, said Marcus. Very good. You'll get the hang of this, I swear. It's just practice. Easy doings. Robert, how about you taking a shot at it?

Lily's husband stood in the corner, rigid, his eyes wide.

+++

An hour later, in their apartment, Lily cried again, when Robert forgot how to set the oven timer and blackened a Stouffers frozen pizza. The smoke alarm had set off the fire alarm and summoned the fire department, so their accident was publicized. Management would surely use it as an example of a "What Not to Do" at the next residents' meeting. Lily and Robert stood next to each other in the courtyard, red-faced, surrounded by everyone else, waiting for the all-clear. Back inside, they ate bowls of corn flakes. The air stank like ash and lodged in every corner of their small apartment.

The assisted-living couples' apartments at Foundation House were modest two-bedroom units with a galley kitchen, a dining area, living room, full bath, and laundry nook. Assigned counselors visited the resident couples weekly to make sure they were keeping up with the routine domestic tasks of shopping and meal preparation, house cleaning, laundry. The counselors checked refrigerators for types and quantities of food. They checked on prescription meds, and the sanitary condition of the bathrooms.

There were twelve assisted-living apartments, four per floor. Located directly opposite from the assisted residence wing was the administrative area and the living quarters for the staff and counselors. A two-story space in the center of the complex housed the common rooms used for recreation and instruction. Outside, the landscaped grounds surrounding the red brick structures were simple but attractive. The residents were invited to care for their own garden beds. Robert and Lily had planted white petunias in May. The flowers looked beautiful for four weeks, struggled onward for six more, then ultimately succumbed to a chronic lack of watering.

Beyond the empty flower beds, at the street, stood a low brick wall with aluminum lettering. Foundation House, Building Better Lives.

+++

Before he could forget the burnt pizza lesson, Robert found some empty space on his left forearm, near the elbow, and wrote PTSMPT. Press Timer, Set Minutes, Press Timer.

There, he said. Next time, no black lunch.

Lily pushed herself from the table and left the kitchen. Robert heard the front door close.

Marcus had told Robert to expect this. When a woman is going to have a baby, said

Marcus, they may act differently than normal. They can cry a lot and yell a lot and go throw up at the oddest times. And that's women who don't even need Foundation House! So, don't you think Lily will need lots of support and understanding? Robert had nodded. Then he had felt like he should write something about that on his left arm, his domestic arm, but he didn't know what to write, so he left some space for it on the inside of the elbow, for when he knew more. Now half of the space was gone, used for PTSMPT.

Both of Robert's arms, wrist to shoulder, were covered in letters. Large, small, blue, black. He looked like he'd been gang-tattooed by kindergartners. The left arm was reserved for Lily and the apartment. On the top of his index finger, between the first and second knuckle: TTOF. Take Trash Out Fridays. On his bicep, in big text: RDFDOM. Rent Due First Day Of Month. He had some numbers, too—Lily's birthday (6/6/83) and their anniversary (9/19/02), almost a year ago. When the baby was born, he'd need to add another number. He checked his arm. There was space for it, on the inside of his elbow, next to PTSMPT. That one had just been added. It had something to do with the kitchen.

Robert's right arm was covered with his work reminders. Foundation House had several established employment programs, and the outreach office had located a job Robert could handle, stocking shelves at the nearby Nature's Bounty market, and every time Robert made a mistake, he took out his marker and wrote another reminder. Diego, Robert's boss, always joked about this. On Robert's first day, on the back of his right hand, Robert had written the letters HAND. Just in case you forget, laughed Diego. Just in case of brain lock, right Einstein?

But the joke was on Diego. HAND didn't mean that, literally. It meant Have A Nice Day. Robert decided he would say that to all the customers. Have A Nice Day. Diego didn't want him talking to customers too much. Just stack the cans, said Diego. But Robert learned things and Robert wrote them down. Like ACED: Always Check Expiration Dates. Then he kept forgetting what "expiration" meant, so under ACED he wrote EMTR: Expiration Means Turning Rotten. He also wrote BTBS. Be The Best Stocker.

Diego could be nice, too. On occasion, he would tell Robert to keep up the good work. Robert was strong and dedicated and maintained an aura of vague athleticism about him. He kept his hair in a neat buzz cut and his Nature's Bounty Market T-shirt was usually clean. If he kept his mouth shut, said Diego, he'd be fine.

Diego told Robert he might turn out to be the most successful Special Eddie they'd ever hired.

+++

For the second time that day, Lily sobbed in her counselor's arms.

I don't want to have a baby, she said. I can't do it.

Do you remember what your parents said when you wanted to marry Robert? said Marcus. Didn't they say it would never work?

He felt her nod against his collarbone.

What did you say to them?

I said we could do it, she whispered. Two are better than one.

That's right, said Marcus. Two are better than one. Because one remembers to feed the dog and the other remembers to let it outside to pee. That's teamwork.

But I'm afraid I'll kill the baby, said Lily.

Well, that's always a possibility, something we'll need to watch, said Marcus.

I need your help, said Lily. Robert can't help. He just can't do it all. And I'll drop it.

Help you do what? asked Marcus. I can help you if you decide you want to keep the baby. I can also help you if you don't. I wanted to make sure you knew that was an option.

Someone can get rid of the baby? said Lily, shocked.

If that's really what you want.

Would it hurt when they do it?

No, you wouldn't feel a thing.

I mean the baby.

I don't know anything about that.

That would be so sad. But you'll help me, right? asked Lily. Please, Marcus?

I always help you, Lily, said Marcus. Don't I always help you?

Sometimes I wish I was married to you instead of Robert, said Lily. You would be a good dad. I mean, I guess you both would. I mean, Robert would be good at some things. He would be good at playing blocks with the baby and stuff, but you would always know what to do when the baby got sick. That's more important.

Maybe now is just not the right time for a baby, said Marcus. I think in a few years, you and Robert will learn a lot more and you could probably be good parents. In a few years.

Lily thought that made sense. Right then, it seemed so impossible to be a parent, especially for people like her and Robert. It was even too hard for lots of smart people, like Lily's own parents, who had wanted a girl so badly for so long that all of that intensity must have harmed their fetus. Both of them, particularly her mother, had already dreamt out a script for a daughter and a corresponding series of wardrobe changes, from ballet tutus to equestrian outfits to pompoms and graduation robes, and the child they finally had fit the physical description, right down to blonde hair and dimples, but things derailed quickly when the girl wouldn't speak in normal words. Little Lily howled, moaned, grunted. They learned her non-verbals as best they could. Not unheard of, the specialists said. Quite commonplace, actually, in the developmentally disabled.

How her parents hated that phrase, fired any specialist who dared speak it, because it felt dirty and treacherous and weighed more than they were prepared to carry. How do you calculate the energy necessary to navigate years of stares and whispers, all the awkward questions, the short yellow buses waiting at the end of the driveway, the decades of dependency? The answer is that you don't. You can't. You resort to instinct instead—instinct to nurture, or instinct to run.

+++

When Robert and Lily first found out that Lily was going to have a baby, just months after they got married, Marcus asked Robert to remember his own childhood, and how it made him feel. Marcus sat ready to write on his clipboard. Robert floundered. He could not remember his parents at all. He'd always imagined them this way: a father tall and full of distractions, a mother brown-eyed and sad. He could hardly recall the county youth facility; nothing came to mind but hallways full of flickering fluorescent tubes and that awful smell, the stench of piss and bleach. He remembered nothing from his years with the first two adoptive families. Those chapters were totally blank. Marcus said that maybe that part was blank because it wasn't so good and the human mind tends to forget the bad things so they can't keep hurting us.

Robert did remember a handful of happy things, eventually, and Marcus wrote them down. He liked the dog at the third family's house. It was a black Lab, Roscoe, or maybe it was Russell, and Robert would rub its belly every chance he got and the dog would lick his face. He remembered a telescope he got once, for Christmas. With it, on clear nights, he could see the dark lakes on the surface of the moon and decided to go wade in them himself until his third fake father laughed and told him to never mind that nonsense, you had to be smart to be an astronaut.

+++

On many nights, Robert and Lily couldn't sleep. Each could tell the other was awake by their breathing, quick and shallow.

On one particular occasion, in the darkness, Robert turned on his pillow and said, do you like Marcus more than me?

Not more, she said.

+++

When the small hand of the clock on the kitchen wall pointed right at five, and Lily hadn't returned, Robert put on his jacket and pulled the hood tight over his head because of the rain. He dodged the puddles all the way down West Clifton Boulevard and turned right onto Sloane Avenue, to the market. He waved hello to Diego and bought a few groceries with his employee discount, including one of those pre-cooked rotisserie chickens. He wanted Lily to have a good meal. And the baby, too, of course. Chicken was good for unborn babies. All that protein, because their little bodies were under construction. Muscles need protein. He told the shoppers that sometimes, at the market: buy our chicken, it's good, lots of protein! Then Diego would tell him to shut up and stack the cans, but Robert would still call out Have A Nice Day.

+++

Marcus slowed the car and pulled over to the curb in front of the clinic, windshield wipers pumping furiously. Lily was silent, her hands wringing the sweater she held in her lap, covering up the slight bulge in her belly that had just started to swell during the last two weeks. Her long hair was stuffed beneath a Cleveland Indians cap. Dark circles framed her eyes.

So beautiful, thought Marcus, but so careworn. This would be the better thing for her, and it was his job to make things better for her, especially considering the circumstances.

Marcus was a senior counselor and he liked his job, wanted to keep it. He was good at it. Not perfect, but good. He had helped a lot of people along the way. He had also made mistakes over the last ten years; some severe, most of them unintentional, a few that had caused him real trouble, but never one that threatened to leave a spreading wake behind like this. Distance would help. Several states between them would help. His résumé was out and already generating inquiries. He had some vacation time coming, saved up for interview trips.

Are you okay? Ready to go in? he asked.

Lily nodded. Water thrummed against the top of the car and ran in waves down the car windows, flung sideways by the wipers, turning the city into a series of split-second watercolor renderings.

Lily turned. Marcus, this won't hurt any of the future babies, right?

Not a chance, said Marcus. Everything will be fine. The doctors here handle this kind of thing all the time. Easy doings.

Lily opened her door and stepped out into the rain.

+++

Robert sat at the kitchen table. He'd tried to avoid eating any of the chicken, and yet one wing was now missing and Robert's fingertips were greasy. He promised himself he would not touch the rest until Lily came back. He sat on his hands. His listened to his stomach make angry noises.

Order had been failing him lately. Robert relied on order to navigate his days, breaking life down into manageable tasks with distinct sets of directions to follow—life as a series of a thousand different little instruction manuals, and that process had served him well, at least until now. There was no checklist for this situation; the logic of his current dilemma escaped him. He knew that it took a man and a woman to make a baby, he knew the basic mechanics, but in their case, there still seemed to be a few pieces missing. He and Lily had not had actual sex on their wedding night (actual sex as he understood it to be), because they had both returned to Foundation House a little drunk and had collapsed into bed too happy and too exhausted to do anything but sleep. They tried on subsequent nights, and things seemed to start off well enough, but it usually came to an end without him actually being inside of her. He'd asked Marcus about it once, and Marcus said he would help, but there was Robert, still waiting. Robert had left some space open on his arm to write the steps for whatever it was he was missing—there was a blank area near the PTSMPT on the inside of his left elbow. Marcus had told him to be patient, that he'd get to him soon, but he was busy helping Lily first. Sometimes Lily would spend all her counseling time with Marcus in his apartment, in the other wing, and when she came back home, she seemed different to Robert, like she'd learned too much at once and it was all wedged up tight inside her brain.

+++

In the waiting room, Lily fidgeted in a plastic chair while Marcus spoke with the woman at the window. Lily thought about what she would say to Robert. He would be sad at first, but maybe he would come to understand that the two of them could not handle a child. Or anything else important, really. Two are no better than one if the two are only halves to begin with. That math won't work. Lily needed more than that. She would tell Robert that she wanted to be with Marcus. Then she would tell Marcus that she wanted to live with him instead, and if they were to have a baby, she and Marcus, then she wouldn't be so scared next time.

+++

The woman at the window asked Marcus if he was the father.

I'm just a counselor, he said, shifting his weight. From Foundation House.

The woman nodded, typed something into her file.

Marcus toyed with the car keys.

Just here trying to help out, he added.

Just here to assist.

+++

When Lily's parents turned her out of their house, the day she turned eighteen, they'd given her one-hundred dollars cash and a piece of paper with the address for a non-profit agency that they said could help her get established. She walked across town, far past Kamm's Corners, stopping every block to ask for directions, hungry and confused—after all, a hundred dollars could buy a bus ticket, too. She passed a market, went inside. She picked out two bagels and a bottle of apple juice, letting the piece of paper flutter to the floor. Which way to go, she thought. East? South? Someplace else, full of people who needed help, she decided, and full of their helpers.

Somewhere I might stand a better chance of finding my way.

A young man tapped her shoulder, handed her back the scrap of paper. It was what he said, and the way he really meant it, that made her believe nice days could be had by someone like her.

+++

Robert stared at the roasted chicken. Sitting there on the table, brown skin taut, without its wings, it reminded him of the doll from earlier that morning. Instinctively, Robert grasped the drumsticks in his left hand, lifted the chicken, and slid his right hand under it, all the way to the end. If the chicken's limp head were still attached, it would have lay cradled in the middle of Robert's outstretched palm. Robert smiled wide. He would show the trick to Lily, and then everything would be fine. Look, Lily, he'd say, no clues even. No broken egg. See, we'll be fine! Our baby will be okay and grow up strong and be so smart, way smarter than Diego, maybe even as smart as Marcus, and she'll do whatever she can dream up to do and have nothing at all written on her arms and she'll be so happy that she won't mind having two parents as dumb as us.

+++

Lily returned after dark. Robert heard the key in the lock, heard the door shut, but she did not come into the kitchen. He found her huddled in bed, beneath a mound of blankets. He forgot about the chicken and sat next to her, silent, for an hour, until they both neared sleep.

Robert remembered what Marcus had told him, about what to expect, the erratic emotions. Thank God for Marcus, he thought, yawning. He and Lily and the baby and Marcus. That is how they'd make it, each supporting the other, like the rickety poles of a tent frame. TSSF. Together, Stand; Separate, Fall.

He smiled in the darkness because he'd thought up that one all by himself.

Terms and Conditions

"Ron, get over here," Morrie said, between coughs, as soon as I answered the phone.

Morrie only called when he had something suitable to impress me with, and since he wasn't an impressive guy by nature, going ten months with no Morrie calls was not an unusual thing.

"What the hell have you been up to?" I asked.

"Busy. Feeling like shit, exhausted, mainly just busy," he said, and hung up.

Morrie was a programmer for some accounting-software firm in Beachwood, one of the pricey suburbs east of Cleveland. He looked more software than accounting—forty, thinning on top, long hair in the back, bifocal lenses. He wore T-shirts and jeans to the office. Morrie had money, pulling in six figures, and since he had nothing but the rent payment putting a dent in it, it had accumulated handsomely. He was an intelligent guy, of course, degrees out the ass, yet not very smart. I tried to explain the difference to him once: *In Brooklyn,* I said, *where I grew up, intelligent might pay the hospital bills, but smart keeps you out of the hospital in the first place.*

Morrie buzzed me into his building, and when the elevator opened at the fourth floor, there he was, waiting for me. "You're about to meet my wife," he said, waiting for his words to register. I stopped in the elevator entrance. It was a fact that Morrie never dated, never got women. We used to joke that the only way he would ever get married would be to—

Holy shit. Holy blessed shit. Morrie, that asshole, had actually gone through with it, with the whole mail-order-bride thing.

Don't get me wrong, it wasn't totally inconceivable; he'd had hundreds of shit-brained ideas, but he usually pulled the plug before he got himself into serious trouble, like the time he convinced himself he could win huge on Jeopardy. He had plunked down $29.95 plus shipping for some three-DVD trivia study kit off the Internet, devoured the things, bugged me relentlessly to ask him questions. *C'mon*, he said, *anything…U.S. Vice Presidents. Victorian Literature. Famous Ivans.* I ignored him. *You think Trebek will like me?* he asked. *Not a chance*, I told him. *Hell, I don't even like you most of the time.*

According to Morrie, he had taken delivery of Katya five months before, and she hadn't left the apartment since.

Morrie opened the door. A woman was waiting there, large-framed, muscular, no stranger to work. Short blonde hair. Nervous eyes, the tell-tale sign of spinning gears.

She nodded to me, slightly, face level with mine.

"Katya's from Russia," said Morrie. "Bigger than I thought, too. Someone in Russia must know Photoshop."

"No Russia. Kazakhstan," snapped Katya, with a scowl.

"Oh, right, Kazakhstan," sneered Morrie. "Kurdistan, Pakistan, Dumbfuckistan—they're all the same, right? Mud huts and goat-humpers."

I sidestepped Morrie's mess, found my own opening. "So, Katya, what did you do there, back in Kazakhstan?"

She looked at me, puzzled. "Do? Do? I live. Live in Kazakhstan."

"No," I said, "I mean…work. What kind of work?"

"I help with…farm…animals…doctor," she said, with considerable difficulty.

"Like a veterinarian's assistant?" I asked. Too fast, I realized, slowing it down. "You—

helped—with—surgeries?" I pretended to slice my abdomen open with the edge of my hand.

She jabbed a finger into her shoulder. "Yes, I help…like this." She rested her head on that same shoulder, eyes closed.

"But here in America," Morrie scoffed, "she washes a few dishes, does some laundry, watches Oprah, opens her little care packages with all those vials and powders and worthless concoctions her friends send her. What a fucking waste."

"Okay," I said to Morrie, "so you get her signed up for some internship training, some tutoring with English, and then she can go do anesthesia in a pet clinic somewhere. Get her out of the apartment, bring in some extra cash."

Morrie laughed, shaking his head. "Are you kidding me? She can't give a blowjob without a manual. What the hell do you think she'd do with all those drugs? We don't use that herbal crap of hers here in the civilized world. She'd be out on her ass after Day One. Complete with lawsuits, for Christ's sake. A dead pet is serious shit here, pal, not like Kazakhstan; it's just another meal to those fucking Omars, isn't that right, Katya? No, she's gonna stay right here, aren't you, babe? Wash those dishes and wait for Daddy to come home from work."

Katya gave him a middle-fingered stare and disappeared into the kitchen.

Morrie sat at the dining room table. I followed. He looked anemic in the late afternoon light filtering through the old leaded-glass windows. He looked warped, uneven, like the glass itself.

Morrie shook violently, moaned in pain, then yelled, "Damn it, Katya, get us some tea." He leaned toward me and muttered, "I'm seriously thinking of returning that bitch."

"You can do that?" I whispered, amazed.

Morrie nodded, tapping a finger against his temple. "I went and bought the warranty, see. One-year limit on the return, no questions asked. Incompatibility, false advertising, whatever. Any reason at all. Send her back, get a new one." He reached over to a small desk next to the table, grabbed a catalog and tossed it on the table in front of me.

I thumbed through it. It had a solid black cover, and was indexed by continent and country. Inside were glossy thumbnail photos and short bios of hundreds, maybe thousands of women, from every second- and third-world nation you could imagine. It reminded me of those used car publications you pick up for free at the supermarket check-out: *Low miles. Runs great. All offers considered.* I pushed it back at him, both intrigued and repulsed. "Can't you do this crap online?" I asked.

"Sure, the catalog's just for effect," he replied, jerking his thumb toward the kitchen.

"So how would that work, exactly? A return, I mean."

"Simple," said Morrie, "I scan and email them a copy of the divorce papers, she loses her green card, I take her to Customs at Newark and put her on Lufthansa, airfare prepaid, return to sender, bye-bye Katya." He said that last part louder, toward the kitchen, then smiled. "And then I pick a new girl."

I thought for a moment. "And what options does she have?"

Morrie shrugged. "Beg me, I guess, suck up to me, try to get me to change my mind. If they get returned, they forfeit the escrow money they were due, and that sucks big time because most of them do it to help their families in the first place."

"And you wouldn't feel bad about that? At all?" I said.

"Hell no!" said Morrie. "Her worst day here beats the best day she ever had in Crap-shack-istan. No, she's stuck. She can't do a thing."

Katya had appeared in the doorway with a silver tray and two china cups. Morrie stared at her, but continued to speak to me. "I'm thinking Korean this time. What do you think? They're bound to be smaller."

Katya approached the table. Instinctively, I reached for a cup. In one motion, she set the tray down hard and swatted my hand clear of the tea. Her eyes were molten, and in them I smelled smoke, and behind them I could see across the frozen stubble of a spent wheat field at dusk, toward a weathered farmhouse, and on into its dim recesses, where an old man hunched over an iron stove, nursing smoldering coals whose faint heat was already swallowed up by the bitter night.

"Cup with spoon is his," said Katya, pointing to Morrie, and offering it to him. The remaining tea, mine, had no spoon.

Katya sat next to the window. Morrie drank. I didn't. The room grew quiet. A radiator began to clank somewhere in the apartment. We listened to it. Minutes passed. Fifty-three clanks.

I heard a new sound, a buzzing, coming from nearby. Katya was watching a fly trapped between the outer screen and the glass. When it alighted, near the bottom of the screen, she raised the inner sash a few inches.

"Shut the goddamn window, I'm freezing here!" snarled Morrie. He shuddered again, lurched forward, cupping his tea in both hands and pressing it to his forehead. Every bit of color had left his face.

I watched Katya shut the window, most of the way.

Armored

The only real superhero I know lies sandwiched between blue and green tarps beneath the northbound lanes of the Fulton Avenue Overpass, ever since last winter's screaming winds drove him, sonofabitching, into the pigeon-shitted ass-crack of the concrete bridge abutment. Just because a man has some powers doesn't mean he won't feel the burn of frigid wind on bare skin when he whips it out to take a January-morning piss. He's still a man, for Christ's sake. There's no chance of life letting Charles forget that. They have an apparent understanding, those two. Charles always wins in split decisions, but life gets its body shots in, without fail.

Twice a week, I bring Charles peanut butter sandwiches, cups of chicken soup, bad coffee. In return, he tosses me the dried crusts and gnawed rinds of his stories: *Metairie. Mama Rose. 'Nam. McNeeley.* I scoop them up and pocket them, trusting they'll amount to something. (I remember reading once, in *National Geographic*, how archaeologists found fragments of papyrus scrolls in the tomb of the pharaoh Ramesses. There weren't enough of them to make sense of.

It could be a royal edict, one of the scientists said, *or it could be a shopping list.*)

Charles wears his many garments like chainmail. The outermost layers are vests—visible, accessible—so this is where I begin:

Vest #1, faded orange, was 1959, and Charles, maybe you were nine-years-old, and you kept your fears where you could see them, on a piece of scrap paper in your back pocket. Water was top of the list, because in Metairie, either the lake was rising or the levee was crumbling, so you hid a Navy surplus lifejacket under your mattress for when the time came. Maybe your real mama was dead, so you lived with your auntie, Mama Rose, and her man Mr. Delbert, who always looked at you funny. That time he drove you out to Lake Ponchartrain to do a little fishing, *just us boys*, you had the vest on underneath your shirt. Maybe when he parked the rusty sedan on the embankment, that's when you realized he didn't bring any gear? And when he started touching you where you didn't like, you said you'd go tell Mama Rose, and he got out. He jumped out and pushed, and when the car rolled down and hit the surface, you looked out the rear window and watched him until the brown water rose up and left you in dark and quiet.

Vest #2, camouflage, was July 1969, the Mekong Delta. The steam of midday was asphyxiating—but you, Charles, you kept your flak vest on just in case. Maybe the L.T. put McNeeley on point that day (big fucking mistake, because his head was still sucked full of weed), and he stumbled right through a Vietcong tripwire. McNeeley was instantly pulverized; Gomez, who was second in line, lost half his limbs. Maybe you, Charles, were third, and you were thrown twenty feet into a grove of bamboo, and you regained consciousness with a sizzling hunk of shrapnel lodged in your flak vest, just inches from your heart. The scar, by campfire light, looks like a question mark.

Vest #3 is reflective, like tinfoil. Maybe it was just a year or two ago, Charles, when you slouched in the doorway of some electronics store after closing time, and the new flat screen TVs were turned up so loud that you heard the news anchor talking through the glass about *Dangers From Above*, threatening those who spent significant amounts of time outdoors. *Ultraviolet rays*, the man said, *Ozone holes. Satellite bursts of electromagnetic radiation.* Maybe you crouched deeper into the alcove and coughed up phlegm speckled with crimson and felt for your back pocket, for your list.

Charles listens to me, motions to me for another peanut butter sandwich. I go get one out of the van and return, partially displaying it from the pocket of my coat like a dealer might. Charles knows the drill. *Angola Penitentiary*, he says, and my mind is already running to Charles cornered in the exercise yard, a crude shiv to his gut, lots of blood, but no vital organs. Charles takes the sandwich from my outstretched hand and eats half. He takes the remaining portion, wraps it carefully in newsprint, and puts it in a dented steel toolbox for Loud Annie.

Loud Annie visits him sporadically, wordlessly. She seems younger than Charles, in an indeterminate way. Loud Annie, too, is redacted; her blacked-out sections are urban camouflage, movable graffiti, and conceal her descent into Charles's camp like a fog stealing in off Lake Erie. She brings him soiled coats and blankets, harvested from God-knows-where. Charles doesn't always keep them, but he always gives Annie the sandwiches, and she always grins in return. I've imagined other, clandestine transactions—kisses, perhaps, or sex. I approach that mental image cautiously, like a crime scene. Charles has his vests on, while his bare black ass rises and falls, and Vest #3 flashes silver in the moonlight. Loud Annie's moans pile up in her throat, but the logjam dissolves by morning when they both awaken, shivering, listening to the thrum of rush hour in the purple twilight above them, and maybe that's when he finally splits open and bathes them both in his glistening inner things.

Fox, Raven, Rabbit, R.

There is a place deep in the woods where they aren't supposed to go, so of course they go there. They are young. That is important to know. Young and invincible and high on the shimmer in their veins. If their parents truly did not want them to go there, the parents should have said something like: sure, go there, it's fine, go there often if you want.

That kind of parental approval would have snuffed out the very thought of it.

But these parents aren't the brightest. Not stupid, mind you, but simple—and actually about as smart as animal parents would be. Don't go to that place in the woods, they said, and felt like good parents when they said it.

The little fox, the little rabbit, and the young raven encourage each other as they thread their way through thick oak and dense pine.

It will be fine, they say.

The place deep in the woods does not look frightening; quite the opposite. It is a circular clearing in an otherwise solid patch of forest, allowing thin strands of sunlight to reach the ground and ripen the wild blackberries that cluster the thickets in the center. Blackberries are irresistible to young foxes. Young rabbits and ravens too.

It acts on them slowly. They eat and eat, feed each other, laugh as they smear purple stains across the fur and feathers of each other's faces. The more they eat, the less full they feel. They dance to forget about eating, dance until they can't. By now, the thin strands of light have swung around the clearing. The three fall asleep.

When they awaken, it is already dark. Little Fox gathers dry branches. Little Rabbit finds dry grass for tinder. Little Raven finds a flint. They make a fire, but the fire makes them think of food. They are starving. They want to stuff their mouths, their beak with rocks to make it stop. They'd eat the fire if they could.

I want meat, howls the fox, staring at the raven. Raven's breast is thick with muscle.

I want meat, cries the raven, staring back. Fox's hind quarters look full and juicy.

Rabbit is silent, her mouth stuffed with milkweed leaf. By the time she thinks to run, it doesn't make any difference.

+++

(This is a story I wrote for Doctor Isaacson. He kept pressing me, and I admit to getting a bit snippy with him, but he helped me realize something.)

(A small confession: there is no raven. I guess I embellished a bit. I suppose I added the raven because it helps diffuse the tension and what happened after. Doctor Isaacson says that's normal.)

+++

In truth, it's just the little fox and the little rabbit. They wake up in the clearing at dusk and they are starving. The fox gathers the branches and the rabbit gathers the grass, but there is no raven to find any flint. That's just great, they say, no fire for us! They stare at the shine of each other's eyes in the dark.

I want meat, howls the fox.

I want leaves, cries the rabbit. She spies some nearby and stuffs her mouth.

Lucky you, moans the fox.

We can go try to find you some meat, mumbles the rabbit, between munches.

They stumble around the edges of the forest for an hour or more, hoping to trip over a sleeping fawn or lazy opossum, but nothing. Little Fox is ravenous. He even uses that very word—ravenous.

Rabbit laughs weakly. Hey, we should have brought Raven along, she says. You could have eaten him.

Little Fox doesn't say anything. His breathing has gotten heavy. Some kind of haze drops over his eyes.

By the time the rabbit thinks to run, it doesn't make any difference.

+++

(This version feels like progress. Doctor Isaacson has helped me reach the point where I can say with reasonable certainty that there were no animals involved at all—the animals being purely symbolic. The human brain does this type of thing sometimes, to protect us. Doctor Isaacson now has me concentrating on what these animal symbols could mean. If perhaps they might represent real people.)

+++

Let's try this again.

There is indeed a woods and a clearing, near the high school. I take R. to the woods that night after the football game and there are some other guys there: Kyle's friends from our rival school, and they act pretty cool despite the fact that we just kicked their ass all over the field, 54-21 or something like that. R. has a football jersey knotted above her bare navel, her tight ass wedged into tight jeans, hair pulled back in a ponytail, purple lipstick. Someone has weed. Someone else has pharm. Everyone has beer. There is a bonfire that some girls are dancing around on one side and guys are pissing into on the other.

I lose track of time. I swallow a yellow pill with a mouthful of warm beer and then it feels at one point like the whole clearing is lifting out of the ground and floating upward, cruising the sky like a parade float. I pass out in a camp chair.

When I wake up, I go looking for R. In truth, I have a couple of nasty thoughts lurking in the shrubbery of my subconscious. I ask around. One girl who is still coherent points to the edge of the woods. It's dark, far from the fire, but I can make out a blanket on the ground and a girl is lying still on the blanket and a guy on top of her, maybe a guy from the other school, and his pants are down around his ankles and he's riding the girl, piston-like. I know it's her, don't ask me how. I feel like running, but all I can do is vomit down my front.

+++

(That Doctor Isaacson, I have to give him credit. At this point, he suggests maybe we go visit the clearing in the woods, as some sort of grounding exercise, and I hesitate. I'm not sure why I do that. We explore my reluctance, for several sessions. Summary: as it turns out, there is no woods. No clearing either.)

(Doctor Isaacson is now questioning my recollection of the past.)

+++

Maybe it wasn't high school, he suggests. Could it have been earlier?

No, I say, no way, Doc. I know what I saw.

Then maybe later? College?

Well, yeah, I guess it could have been college. Back at Wittenberg. That makes some sense.

Okay, good, let's follow that thread. College. What comes to mind?

+++

There is a frat party, the first of the year for Sigma Chi. It's a big deal. It always gets way out of hand. It's the kind of party that parents warn their daughters about. Don't go alone, they say, go in a group, watch out for each other, don't drink anything that you didn't see being served. And their daughters nod their heads, thinking all the while that these parties must be really awesome to warrant such a warning.

The girls encourage each other as they thread their way through the sweaty crowd and the thumping bass.

R. is there with some of her freshman friends, a large clot of estrogen coagulating around the keg. Rads, the Sig Chi social officer, is filling the plastic cups, chatting the girls up.

I've known R. since high school but she's never really noticed me. Not the way a guy wishes to get noticed by a girl, anyway.

Hey, guess what, there is a clearing in the trees after all! It's behind the Sig Chi house and that's where the fire pit is and I'm the lucky pledge candidate on fire duty. I drink a lot and bullshit a lot and I watch R. when she comes out to warm up by the fire. The light glistens in her eyes. She goes inside, and I fall asleep in a camp chair.

Sometime later I wake up and the fire has burnt way down.

I go inside looking for R. I find her passed out on the couch in Rads' room. Her jeans are unzipped and the buttons on her blouse are out of alignment by one. I wait for an hour in the dark, then wake R. and walk her back to her sorority. I keep saying I'm sorry. Rads is an asshole. He'll be gone in eight months. Please don't report this. Please don't ever come back to Sig Chi house.

+++

(Doctor Isaacson is asking me why I'm biting my lip and digging my nails into my thighs as I tell this story.)

(Now he wants to know if I'm doing it again.)

Doing what?

Kevin, is Rads real? Or is he like the raven from before?

(I'm pissed now. Seriously, what kind of a question is that?)

Kevin, please describe Rads to me.

I close my eyes so I can picture him better. He's kind of tall, I say.

And?

Looks a little older than me.

What about his hair? What color? Long or short?

I'm thinking. He just looked...average. Dark hair.

Black hair?

Maybe.

Kevin, can we go meet Rads? Talk with him? Do you know how to contact him?

+++

Wait, hold on, black. Black hair, yes, I'm thinking, black as midnight in a deep wood with no fire, black as raven feathers, storm clouds, dorm rooms, oh god, oh my god, oh god no. No one. No one else. No Rads. There was no Rads! Only me. Just me and R. and the pills and the alcohol and the thumping bass and her slumping over and her never paying attention to me and me feeling the voltage in my veins and me locking the door and me pulling her bra off and me pulling her jeans down and me entering some kind of trance that I weave in and out of until I finally clear the fogbank and then it's me panicking and me dressing her and me waking her and me walking her home, telling her a story. Oh god. Fuck. It's me.

+++

(Doctor Isaacson is not saying anything. He's just sitting there.)

I feel like my brain is burning. My heart is pumped dry and cavitating.

(Doctor Isaacson is asking if R. was perhaps younger than I remember.)

(He wants to know if maybe R. is a relative?)

I feel like I should run, but it won't make any difference.

Excerpts from Melroy Mobile Entertainment's New Carnival Worker Orientation

Tilt-A-Whirl

After you've double-checked the shoulder belts and door latches, slowly increase the rate of spin to 45 rpm. When you reach 45 rpm, raise the tilt angle to 35 degrees. After three minutes, reverse the procedure.

If the control wiring comes undone again, re-wrap it with duct tape.

If it is wet, do it anyway.

In case of emergency, hit the red button.

If the red button fails, throw yourself into the gear mechanism.

That last part was a joke. Don't do that. Throw the power disconnect switch and the ride will slow on its own.

The safety of our customers is our top priority.

We think about your safety, too, if it helps you to think that we think that.

Ferris Wheel

Situation: The taller of the two teenage girls smiles at you. It is not your thin body, your high hairline, your crooked teeth, your tattooed hands on the controls. It is not what you think. Her body is on display, granted, but her body is for quarterbacks, frat boys, lawyers—in that order. Never for you. That is what the smile means. You can smile back, if you want, to show that you understand the rules. Just once, though. Not twice. That would be creepy.

Sidenotes

1. We pay in cash, on Sunday nights, after breakdown and load-up.

2. Names are optional; nicknames are mandatory.

3. After each pay call, we read the nicknames going to our next location. If you are on the team, see you there. If your nickname is not read, goodbye. You can keep the T-shirt.

4. We keep no lists. Lists are for registered voters, taxpayers, annual contributors, convicted felons, next of kin. It is assumed that if you are here, you concur.

Three Tries for a Dollar

It is theoretically possible to win the giant stuffed dog. Extremely theoretically, mathematically possible. Someone did once. Repeat: someone did *once*. It is more probable that no one at this carnival will leave with anything worth anything. That, you do not say. Your job is to make things seem more possible than they are. You are selling hope. Yes, a carny selling hope! Such wonderful irony. When the illiterate are allowed to print books for the blind, where is the structure in that? Where are the safeguards? There are holes in this script so big that even we can exist, friend, all balanced on the head of the giant stuffed dog. On the *once*.

Dr. Bizarro's Funhouse

Situation: After the crowds have left, while Fat Brenda runs shutdown, you switch on the housekeeping lights and stare into the wavy mirror. The veterans say that where you stand makes all the difference. You can look taller, shorter, fatter, thinner—just move. You've tried every angle, but you cannot find your spot. It can't do unaddicted, unfelonied, un-unwanted. Are you surprised? Did you think you would find real magic here? Here is where the veterans laugh—wake up, newbie asshole! This is exactly why you are where you are, working for Melroy. Wavy mirrors are made for those who don't need them. For the rest of us, it's back on shift at ten a.m. Try to get some sleep.

Mr. Yard Sale

Walter Eldridge learned a great many lessons during the last few months of his former life, chief among them:

The Russian Mob operating in the Midwest was persistent, nicely dressed, and not above shopping on Craigslist.

The human pancreas does indeed have a purpose. (Corollary for schoolchildren: sixth grade health class likewise has a purpose.)

Wealth, on paper, is still governed by the same forces that govern paper. Paper burns. Paper tears. Paper and wealth, when put to any real test, have no permanence.

Ethel Schweitzkopf would have been proud of him.

A last resort can hide something behind its back.

Walter repeated the list of these lessons in his head, as if repetition might delay their escape into the ether. It was hard, trying to concentrate above the loud cracks made by the splintering of his front door. The Russians would be pushing against the armoire next, budging it just enough to get an arm inside, and then a leg past the jamb, for better leverage.

Thank God he hadn't sold the armoire. He couldn't remember why, exactly. Most people in his situation would have. It was walnut (solid walnut frame, veneer on the doors), Chippendale cornice, claw-and-ball front feet, oil-rubbed bronze hardware. It weighed a freaking ton. Maybe that's why? Because he couldn't move it if his life depended on it, at least until his life actually did depend on it?

He could hear the Russians, on the front porch, shouting in Russian. Or Anglo-Russian. The Anglo-words were all four-lettered and ugly, and despite the Russians' heavy accents, their pronunciation was excellent.

Walter had barricaded himself inside the master bath, perched on the edge of his spa tub. Correction: the bank's spa tub, formerly known as his. Even so, no call for an avoidable mess, right? Someone would have to clean it up, someone whose job sucked so bad that they almost weren't thankful to still be employed. Maybe someone quite a bit like him.

And this is exactly how things would have ended, had Walter Eldridge not done something completely unexpected.

+++

Before the market crash, back before the lay-offs and the bill collectors calling at dinner time and the repo men lurking in the driveway, Walter had achieved a certain level of success in the ways most people measured success: an office with three real walls and a fourth made of glass (non-operable); 4-bed-3.5-bath Tudor colonial in the suburbs; a luxury vehicle with Bluetooth functionality and leather seats; a senior job title. Walter was (*was*) Director of Development for Langston Kelleher Properties, retail developers well known in the industry for creating faux-historical shopping destinations out of cornfields and swampland. Walter had been responsible for creating The Shoppes at Kennesaw, which had graced the cover of *Modern Retail* magazine in Spring 2006, the urban-reclaimed Old Stockyard Market District in Omaha, too, and Three Palms Collection near Orlando. Before September of 2008, these were the places the wealthy spent themselves into a state of euphoria. In retail lingo, these were high end "lifestyle centers," catering to anyone whose style of living was fueled by pomegranate martinis and country club soirees. Langston Kelleher centers appeared like dandelions across the suburban landscape during those headiest of times for capitalists. In those days, no one thought to put down their twenty-dollar drinks and watch for a cliff ahead. The Dow Jones fell three-thousand points in an eye-blink and terrified consumers stopped buying and shell-shocked retailers stopped expanding and Langston Kelleher stopped building and Walter Eldridge stopped being useful.

Don Burkhardt, Vice President of Assets, looked like he hadn't slept since the Lehman Brothers collapse. Was that stubble on his chin? Walter wasn't sure he should sit for this, but there he was, sitting anyway. Don pushed an envelope toward him. "I wish it could be more," he said, "but we're hurting bad, Walt. Real bad. I'm cutting the whole department today. I might not survive either, and if by some miracle I do, I'll be at half-salary, best case. Better that you get out now, while there are still a few jobs left to be had."

Walter took the envelope, folded it, put it into his pocket unopened. It was very light. Too light. Something so life-dismembering should have felt heavier in his hand.

"There's no other way?" asked Walter. He knew better, but it felt like something that needed to be asked. Like if he asked, maybe Don would reconsider. Like maybe if he just asked, very sincerely, maybe Don would commit to scrounging him up a half-salaried, half-useful position to milk for a few more months, at least to get him past Lindsay's graduation and wedding.

"We've got to sell off centers to meet debt," said Don, grinding his palms into his eye sockets. "We're selling Three Palms first, Walt—fifty cents on the dollar. That's your baby, isn't it? What a great property that is. Was. I'm really, really sorry. This whole thing makes me want to puke."

Walter had seen it before: centers that outlived their usefulness, or were shunned in favor of a glitzier new neighbor, following slow trajectories of neglect until their anchors pulled out and the junior-tenant storefronts went dark and their historic-looking park benches traded their chic latte-sippers for the shapeless lumps of sleeping homeless. Now Three Palms Collection would become just another fake-stucco ghost town, populated by filthy pigeons and dollar stores.

Walter got up to leave. He extended a hand.

"It's been good working with you."

"I need your key back," said Don.

+++

In Ethel Schweitzkopf's seminal book *The Art of the (Yard)Sale*, Walter had underlined the following passage, despite the fact that the copy he read belonged to the Lakewood Public Library:

"You can tell an amateur's yard sale from five houses away. They all make the same basic mistake—no overarching structure. Cluttered presentation, without a hint of raison d'etre."

Walter knew she was right. The same people who would never dream of trying to sell their four-bedroom colonials without the services of a professional stager seemed to have no problem vomiting the contents of their home onto their front lawn, stapling hand-scribbled notes on telephone poles, muttering half-assed prayers for clear skies come Saturday next. He knew people like this. People like Rick Fulmer, for instance.

Rick Fulmer was a salesman. It didn't matter what he sold; to him or to anyone else. Mostly he sold himself. Sure, he had some money, but he knew all the right social mirror tricks that made his money expand in people's minds. He had good hair and white teeth and he did sit-ups each morning and he did a lot of women in the subdivision. The cul-de-sac gossips knew exactly which ones, and those same gossips became concerned for Walter and they were pretty sure they knew where Walter's wife Meredith had disappeared to during an unexplained twenty-seven-minute absence at last summer's block party, which also went Rick-Fulmer-less for the same twenty-seven minutes.

Rick Fulmer held on to his job throughout the recession. He just switched product lines. He abandoned Risk/Reward and Speculative Markets and concentrated on things that could be described as Safe, or Conservative, or Time-Tested. He sold annuities. He sold panic room kits. He asked Walter, often, if he'd found work yet. Walter shook his head. Then Rick shook his head. It's tough, Buddy, he said. If things get real bad, you can count on me. I'm not so successful that I can't reach into the gutter and pull someone up, he told Walter, with an uncomfortable shoulder punch. I help the helpless. That's just me. That's what I do.

+++

They sold the Lincoln Town Car first. Walter felt nothing. Three weeks later, when two scruffy men arrived to repossess the Land Rover, Meredith cried. That left Walter's first car, the 1988 Plymouth Sundance, as their only mode of transportation. He'd nursed it well past its natural lifespan just so teen-Rob and teen-Lindsay had something to drive around in. The white paint on the hood and trunk had started to molt in 1989, flaking off at highway speed like an automotive psoriasis, and now the top of the car was mostly a shipyard shade of gray primer. The interior was the color of hooker lips. It harbored the ghosts of questionable smells.

Much of the house was empty. Walter had become an expert Craigslister. He knew how to present household goods in favorable lighting. Advertised and sold: three flat screen TVs, the golf clubs, patio furniture. Meredith was mostly gone, too. She'd resurrected her interest in real estate and took the Sundance keys and disappeared evenings and weekends. When she came back, she smelled different, like carpet freshener and leather upholstery. Staccato dinner conversation became the default stand-in for sex.

All this, and still the proceeds weren't enough. A final batch of Lindsay bills was looming, and Walter needed another twelve grand. Ten might do. Maybe eight, in a pinch, with some further belt-tightening. It was the thought of a tightened belt that first gave Walter the idea.

He checked the Craigslist homepage. As he suspected, there was no category for Organ and Tissue classifieds. He'd have to try Medical/Health. He created a second username, just for the new ad. "Mr. Yard Sale" described himself in whole-foods wording. He indicated that he was blood type O Negative. Universal donor.

He hadn't known what kind of response to expect, which was why he was thrilled to get even one call, from a gentleman with a thick accent. The man had difficulty pronouncing "pancreas," but he understood what one was, and he (or his customer, rather) definitely needed one. Money was not an issue. Time was.

+++

Another gem from Schweitzkopf's tome, page 57:

"Don't fear a calendar collision with the impotent attempts of neighbors. Instead, use it to your advantage! Let their traffic, meager as it may be, amplify your success! Your sale, dear reader, will be premeditated and polished and will shine like a jewel of opportunity next to the haphazard and refreshment-less offerings of all the other uninspired, unsuccessful yard salers on your block."

Walter knew that Rick Fulmer's family was planning to piggyback their sale the same weekend as his, but they were a most pedestrian lot and their presentation would look like so much suburban diarrhea compared to his Buy My Life Event. He wondered—would anyone ever catch the double-entendre? Buy bits of my old life, and in so doing, buy me more life? That was just the kind of stuff Ethel Schweitzkopf wrote about. Raising the bar. Taking your sale from blue collar to white collar.

Walter had followed Schweitzkopf's advice and created a yard sale plan, drawn to scale (one inch = ten feet), so he could visualize such factors as customer flow, rest-in-shade opportunities, sun angles vs. reflective surfaces vs. average customer eye levels. His theme was a variation on the classic chronological structure, but had decided to subdivide his belongings into life "eras." Destination: Childhood, for instance, would house the vintage Matchbox cars, the sports trading cards organized in binders, the crates upon crates of vinyl LPs. On the end cap, he'd place his treasured copy of Pink Floyd's *The Wall,* turned on angle so that customers could see where Roger Waters himself had autographed The Judge's bare buttocks with a black Sharpie. Another aisle, called Go Blue, would feature his college trappings from his Ann Arbor days. Single in Chi-Town would (hopefully) liquidate all the bachelor stuff from the attic that Meredith never let him bring into the house, including a pair of double-bass woofers and a perfectly usable waterbed.

The area furthest from the street would showcase Rob's old sports gear and Lindsay's menagerie of orphaned band instruments (three woodwinds, two brass). There was originally room planned for Meredith to utilize, too, but she had wanted no part of the sale. According to Meredith, life resembled a parade of accumulation, which meant that dispersion of one's goods had a disconcerting affiliation with death. Not so, Walter had argued, but to deaf ears. Lindsay would be graduating from John Carroll on May 20th and become Mrs. Josh Nowicki at the end of June, and with her would leave the last reason for Meredith to stay—in the house, or with him. Walter revised his site plan, re-designating Meredith's space for his-and-hers Porta-Johns.

Walter had managed to contact Schweitzkopf's publicist in New York, mostly to let Ethel know she had a huge fan in northern Ohio, but when he mentioned his own upcoming sale, things had taken quite a different turn. Ethel (revealed the publicist) was in development on a new coffee-table book (working title *Sale-ing Across America*), which she intended to be an arts-piece-meets-human-interest gallery of fifty unique and photogenic yard sales, one from each of the fifty states. A photographer and staff writer would travel in from Manhattan the day of Walter's Buy My Life event. Walter Eldridge could, if he played it right, get to represent the great state of Ohio in what was sure to be a milestone in yard sale literature. He would wear his new tie for the portrait photo. He'd order an extra copy of the book, destination Rick Fulmer.

+++

Shortly after his decision to go ahead with the yard sale, Walter had this dream:

It was a hot, sunny day in some sort of meadow. There were little blue flowers hiding everywhere among the taller grasses. There was one single tree, hanging heavy with crabapples. He held some picnic gear in his hands. He was sweating. Lindsay said Right Here, pointed to a scar in the shade. Lindsay had appeared. A scab of fresh-turned earth. He spread the blanket across the soft dirt. There was some sort of animal, more than one, perhaps many, hiding in the grass. They were discussing something, in whispered animal conversations. Their conversations made him nervous. Lindsay, who now looked like a yellow, fatty organ suspended in a jar of liquid, kept repeating how hungry she was. Walter opened the macaroni salad. Ants swarmed up from under the blanket and climbed the jar. Lindsay was very, very hungry. With one hand, Walter swatted ants from the jar. With the other, he spooned elbow macaroni in the open mouth of the container. They sank slowly to the bottom, clouding the liquid in the process. Lindsay yelled I'm still hungry and the ants were climbing again and Walter did not have enough hands. Not nearly enough hands. Sweat erupted in streams from his scalp, flowed down his neck and inside his collar. The animals in the grass barked, but it mostly sounded like laughing. The little blue flowers in the grass were not flowers at all, but eyes. Walter's body had developed dark cavities at some point during the picnic. They were hungry, too. A strong wind blew and crabapples rained down from the tree and Walter abandoned the ants and the macaroni and Lindsay, using both his hands to cram bruised and rotting apples into his ravenous voids.

+++

Saturday the fifteenth of April promised to be clear and warm, no last-minute sun-prayers necessary. Walter awoke before dawn, did ten crisp push-ups, drank strong black coffee, dressed in golf-ish attire and went outside to position and price the sale items. Just as Ethel's chapter on climate had predicted, springtime yard sales located above thirty-five degrees north latitude could not pre-position merchandise the night before the sale due to possible dew risk. In fact, dew lay in wet sheets over everything. Walter dried the tops of the folding tables with a towel from his recently sold golf bag, then broke them down and lugged them, one by one, over to Rick Fulmer's driveway. Rick's stuff was piled on the lawn. As quietly as possible, Walter arranged all of Rick's things in a bastardized version of his own "life eras" scheme. He finished before any of the five Fulmers were awake.

Walter left this note:

Hey Buddy, just repaying the kindness, hope you like it—Walt

Walter took his sale items from his own garage and dumped them in a long, thoughtless heap down his drive. He tried not to feel nauseous. He tried to forget Ethel's principles. He tried his best to forget the recent dinner conversation that caused this horrible and draconian shift in planning. He could not. It played again and again, looping over the loudspeakers in his brain.

Walter: Lindsay, I think I came up with a way to get you that money for the reception.

Lindsay: What? You did?

Meredith: How?

Walter: You're going to think I'm nuts, but it's something I want to do for you.

Lindsay: Did you cash in your Roth?

Meredith: Oh God, no, please not the Roth.

Walter: No, not the Roth. More creative than that. I'm going to sell one of my pancreases. Or is it pancreae? What's the plural of pancreas?

Lindsay: What!?

Meredith: What!?

Walter: I'll get by just fine with one. No worries. I'm in a decent state of health for a guy my age. I eat fiber. Once in a while.

Lindsay: Dad, you dope, you only have one pancreas! There is no plural! You can't sell it—you'll die! That's what makes insulin, so your blood sugar doesn't go nuts. And it makes stomach enzymes, too. Jesus, didn't you know that? How do you think food gets digested?

Walter: Well, I don't think that's quite right, Lindsay. You hear about parents donating one to their sick kids all the time. I've seen those telethons. What about that?

Lindsay: Kidneys, Dad. Those are kidneys. As in, TWO kidneys. Totally different organs.

Meredith: Oh, Walter, what the hell did you do now?

Walter: Are you sure?

Lindsay: I took Human Anatomy last year, remember?

Walter: You got a C minus.

Lindsay: Okay. Whatever. I'm right, Dad. You were really gonna do it, weren't you? Thank

GAWD I'm still living here. You're so clueless. See this? This is why you're not walking me down the aisle. I can't take this stress. It makes my pores erupt. Just look what you've done to my forehead!

Walter: (standing) I've got to go pull that ad.

Meredith: What ad? What ad, Walter? Holy freaking hell, what's happening to this family!?

Lindsay: Unbelievable.

+++

Walter left the dining room and shut the door of his study. He went online, logged in, and deleted the classified. Then he dialed the number he kept in his wallet.

The Russians never answered their cell phone. They would screen calls, listen to messages, then dispose of the pre-paid phones and call back from new ones.

The one Russian that always spoke to him did not believe in greetings. When Walter answered the return call, the Russian said, "How eez our pencreez today? Good, yes? Vee come for pencreez. Soon."

Walter stammered. "Yeah, right, about that. Listen, I'm really sorry, but the deal is off. Tell whomever it is to find another one. I'm very sick, and I'll be needing mine for the foreseeable future. Sorry. Good luck to you."

Silence.

"So vee come for eet, very soon, our pencreez," said the Russian.

Silence.

+++

Shortly after nine in the morning, a steady stream of cars and customers began jockeying for space along Mulberry, parallel-parking all the way back to Glenwillow. Most passed Walter's pathetic sale, lured by the shiny bouquet of foil helium balloons he'd tied to Fulmer's mailbox, or perhaps reeled in by the upbeat Jimmy Buffett classics launched from an iPod dock with speakers he'd set up in the Fulmer's garage. A few strays ended up in Walter's driveway, hesitant, looking over their shoulders, already contemplating an escape from Walter's drab fare. The photographer and writer arrived around ten, in a silver BMW. The photographer got to work immediately, trying a bit too hard to be inconspicuous, while the writer chose to absorb the scene first, experiencing Fulmer's sale as a customer would. Professionals, thought Walter, watching from his lawn chair. How amazing, to almost rub elbows with Ethel's pros. He hoped Fulmer had the presence of mind to reward them both with complimentary lemonade. Moments later, a third figure emerged from the rear seat of the BMW. The older woman stood and contemplated the scene for a minute before melding with the crowd. The short-cropped red hair, the white pants suit—all so recognizable, from the book jacket photos.

+++

Walter's final few thoughts, as Walter:

Meredith would be fine. She was Rookie Salesperson of the Month. She had started jogging again. Rob would be fine. Rob was always fine. That left Lindsay. Lindsay would just have to learn to make due. She might have to move her reception to the VFW hall. Folding tables, folding chairs, so what? What a good lesson for her, heading into marriage—to hell with the trappings of life. Trappings, she would come to learn, are mostly trap.

There was one thing left to do. Walter backed the Sundance down to the foot of the driveway and popped the rear hatch. Inside was a sloppy, hand painted sign that read FREE STUFF. He propped the sign against his mailbox. People headed for Fulmer's extravaganza eyed his sign and his car and his sad driveway full of junk with pity. They smirked. Their imagined thoughts played out in bold fonts, scrolling the marquee behind Walter's eyes.

Walter, his face flushed, climbed back into the Sundance and lurched out into the street, narrowly missing a black Lexus with tinted windows. The car stopped short, tirescreech and hornblare. The rear window slid down. Walter climbed out from his driver's seat.

"Hey, hey you, such terrible fuck you driver, where eez the one called Meester Yard Sell? It eez you, yes?"

Walter, wordless, shook his head, pointing instead toward Rick Fulmer's place.

The Russian flipped Walter off. Walter waved back. The window went up, returning to reflective. The Russians rolled slowly past his yard, maneuvered through the gap left between a Ford Escape and a fire hydrant, and parked across Fulmer's tree lawn. Three men got out. Two of them were black-suited and enormous. The third, smaller and older, carried a leather satchel in one hand and a small picnic cooler in the other.

+++

The man never again to be known as Walter Eldridge did not look back. Armed with full tank of gas and empty bladder, he took Cleveland-Massillon Road south to the overpass. He pulled over on the gravel shoulder, just past the Sunoco. I can be a Rick Fulmer, he thought, but better—armed with Ethel's weapons. I can sell anything to anyone. Watch for me, in a coffee table book coming out later this year. I know, the photo won't look much like me. I'll say I've aged a lot lately. This economy has tested us all. Hey, friend, do you want to hear a funny story about a pancreas?

To his left lay a few million people and the cold Atlantic; to his right, a different few million, and their roughly one-million yard sales stretched like sweet-corn stands across the Plains. He pulled out into traffic, turned right onto the entrance ramp and merged into the eastbound lanes of Interstate 80, trailing a fine dandruff of white automotive paint deep into the hills of Pennsylvania.

+++

From the Foreword of Ethel Schweitzkopf's forthcoming *Sale-ing Across America*:

"Yard sales are an integral thread in the fabric of American life. This is so, I believe, because they are so fundamentally democratic. Flip through these pages. What do you see? So many flavors of people, defined by their places, whether mansions or double-wides wedged inside trailer parks. The places they are now, and places they're headed. People defined by their things. Everyone is in some process of changing, or becoming, and the things follow suit: Walmart to trailer park and Nordstrom's to mansion. Believe it or not, someone out there is trying to be you, wanting your old stuff as their new stuff, while you've got your eyes on another's place and another's belongings. Things are the fuel of our cultural engine. Or are they the emissions? And if the answer is both, doesn't that indicate how much they are ingrained in who we are?

There will be bad days, of course. Possessions will feel like prisons. Rain will fall. No buyers will come. Accepting pennies on dollars will feel like surrender, not survival. But take heart, dear yard saler. Rest assured that someone out there wants what you have. It's a fact. And that is, in the end, the greatest aspect of the American yard sale—the proof of change, which is proof of life.

Tiny Fake Us, Staring Out to Sea

Two days after my son stops talking, he builds a miniature version of our house, rendered in wood scraps, LEGO, milk cartons. A family lives inside: two PLAYMOBIL children (one with a hardhat), plastic cat mother. I am a cork from a wine bottle. I wonder at the message here. I have no limbs. I guess I'll sleep standing up, so as not to sleep-roll off the second floor.

I ask my son if I can play with him. I keep one eye on the evening news. Another suicide bombing in Pakistan.

Nods yes.

"Can I be me?"

Nods yes.

A hospital this time. Legs of children poking from rubble.

Cork Dad: "Hello Son, how was school today? Good?" (Not knowing how a cork dad would talk, I sound vaguely Australian.)

Shakes head no.

"Girl problems? Bullies?"

No.

The anchor has moved on. An FBI child trafficking crackdown here in the Midwest. Fifty-seven arrested in Chicago.

Cork Dad: "It's okay if Real You doesn't want to talk, but maybe Pretend You can talk?" (I'm always doing this—coaxing him from holes. If he were adopted, or a mongoose, it would make more sense.)

"For a little while," he mumbles.

"So, what's bothering you?" I ask. "For a small plastic guy, you seem to have a lot on your mind."

"My teacher says that in a few years, most of Antarctica will melt and Florida will be under water."

The little fake family is huddled on the roof.

"Don't worry," I tell him, "That could be years and years from now. And even if it happened, we'd be safe."

He frowns. "You would. You can float."

"I'd save us all," I say. "You, your hard-hat sister, and Mom Cat, too. I'd scoop you all up and we'd float to higher ground."

"You don't have any arms," he says.

"I have an idea," I say. I take out my pocketknife and slice three discs from Cork Dad. I cut a notch out of each, so they fit like little flotation collars around the necks of the others. "There! Now we'll all survive."

"Those look stupid," he says, frowning. He leaves the room. His footsteps shake the floor, quake the little house. What's left of me rolls off the roof. I have no arms to wave goodbye.

The anchor ends the newscast with a story about a blind high-school senior in Atlanta who finally gets to play varsity soccer thanks to a ball that emits a beeping sound. She follows the sound around like a bat might. Her future looks brighter, her parents suggest—faces unconvinced. The reporter falters; she has no closing. The anchor won't make eye contact with the camera—he keeps looking down, as if there's sea water lapping at his ankles.

Fossils

Fossil me, she says, on a Sunday afternoon when lake-effect snow strikes and shackles everything tight under its belly.

She larvaes in front of the fireplace, cocooned in quilt.

Explain, I answer, watching the flake-fall from my chair. My car has become a tumor beneath thick porcelain skin.

Rediscover me, she says. Search for me, but do your homework first: organize an expedition, hire a local guide, endure hardships, read the strata, hypothesize, then dig. Dig, like nothing else matters.

I've loved you for fifteen years, I say. Without Sherpas. Isn't that expedition?

Long expeditions are deadly, she says, they breed institutions. Discoveries disappear into textbooks.

You want some time away? I ask.

I want to be unearthed again, she says, marveled at, brushed delicately, cradled, magnified, examined, taxonomied, announced at symposiums.

It falls harder, that downy sediment.

Cephalopod or gastropod? I ask her, in that way of mine.

Neither, she says, yawning. Something that flew once, before the sap, and before the amber. A dragonfly, maybe. A careless one.

Ah, no bigger than a grapefruit then, I figure. So how would I find you?

She turns to me. You found me before, she says.

Something in the fire snaps.

We played this game, once:

Me: What's sadder than a shovel buried?

You: A fossil reburied.

Outside, the lump that had marked my car is no longer visible.

We stop talking, to conserve oxygen.

How Cold Wars End

Sunday's supposed to be MY day, my one good day, a couch-nap day, a horizontal/pro football/cold beer balanced on gut day, but today I'll never reach that nirvana stage where my roommate Franz dwells, The Blissful Order of the Empty Head, because my girlfriend Didi says I have to go wage dinner at her parents' place again. "Remember what we planned," she shouts from the bathroom, over the whir of the blow dryer.

But free grub, you say.

Yeah, well, free my ass, I say. Just like the Sioux got free housing at Pine Ridge.

I wait as long as I can, then pull on a clean T-shirt and brush my teeth. Franz is off somewhere with his new piece. She's a realtor. She does Sunday afternoon home showings to roughly three eager young couples a month. She sort of specializes in starter homes, which also work well for empty-nesters. She covers both ends of the spectrum—young couples who can't wait to make kids; older couples who can't wait to ditch them. The rest of the time, she is stuck inside these very clean empty houses with Franz, having echoey sex on black granite countertops in newly renovated kitchens. I don't know how the guy does it. The only money I know he makes is from mowing the lawn at Didi's parents' place, which I hooked him up with, so why he suddenly has big cash falling out of his pockets, I have no idea. Just last night, he was sitting there in front of the big screen, tuning up for drone season. Working on his joystick skills, practicing low-level flying and camera zoom controls. Aerospace industry lobbyists down in Columbus waited until the deer population hit crisis level, then put the full-court press on the legislature and got one week of remote drone hunting inserted between bow season and rifle season, so now Franz and other nature-averse outdoorsmen can bag a buck from the comfort of their living rooms. Seriously, it's big business. Next Wednesday (if he doesn't find an excuse to blow up something by then), Franz is taking the drone in to the shop to swap out the Hellfire missile for a full-swivel gun mount. I asked him why. You can't mount a buck's head on your wall if it's vaporized, he said. Just like Franz—all about the trophies, and no walls to hang them on.

The screen is mostly dark and grainy, except for a few green blips.

"Night mode?" I asked.

"Yeeeeaaaah buddy," Franz said, distracted. "Infrared scanning. Looks like I found me a few venison sacks on the move. Gonna circle back around for a mock strafing pass."

"You sure they're deer?"

"Yup, see there? They move at night, in small groups, single file."

"So do Boy Scouts," I said.

He said nothing, concentrating on keeping his one-and-only drone out of the treetops.

I'm struck by how useless Franz's existence is. How adrift. And how, if I squint and blur my vision, it could be me slumped in that beanbag chair, killing from a different zip code, not even budging my heart rate.

Didi's parents live on the east side of town, in Maple Heights. They would not be half bad if they weren't so time-stuck. Not so wallowing in the kitschy paranoia of 1955. Here's a typical Fifties thing they do—they call Didi by her full name, Dolores. Yes, Dolores: that very popular 1940s girl's name which enjoyed a decade-long run. There are still quite a few of them out there, the remnants of the big Dolores wave, their wheelchairs parked in the day rooms of nursing homes and drooling all over themselves. My Didi looks like 2010 with year-round long sleeves. The sleeves are on account of the scars; the scars on account of the cutting; the cutting on account of the general state of affairs for a younger Didi. Something happened back then that she doesn't want to talk about.

I pull into the parents' driveway. The Davis home shines amidst the worn patches of Maple Heights like a home-school prom queen. This section of the city has reached the point where lawns go un-mowed, where flaccid aluminum gutters hang by a single nail. Years ago, white families settled these streets, fleeing other blackening neighborhoods. Now the wind's changed and they've packed up and moved on again, their rundown bungalows backfilled by black families fleeing entire scorched-earth inner-city blocks lost to drugs and gangs.

Didi's father, Dwight, sits on the front porch, little blooms of pipe smoke hovering inches above his sad comb-over like aborted cartoon thought-bubbles. He eyes my car with disdain. "What's that make again?" he'll ask. "Honda," I'll say. "Those Japs have tiny little everything's, don't they?" he'll say, chuckling. In his mind, it should be fifteen feet longer, have rear fins and a nameplate from Detroit applied by unionized, beer-bellied Americans. He stands in slow motion, like he's in pain, from bad knees or else from seeing me. I see he's got a respectable gut started himself, a first-trimester lasagna-baby bump. I shake his hand firmly. That is important to him. You can tell a lot about a man by his handshake, he always says, same with his shirt. Does the man's grip say confident, trustworthy? Does his shirt say sharp as a tack, employee of the month, making the scene in life? My shirt says NASCAR, Tony Stewart #14, and courtesy of some sticky red stains, Double Diablo hot-wing sauce. Damn, I could have sworn I washed this one. I need to be more disciplined with the ol' clothes piles. That method works best in college, when everyone else does the clothes piles, too. Ah, college: dirty laundry equilibrium.

Didi's parents' house looks like the house in the old *Leave It to Beaver* television show, except that instead of suburban quaint, it's satanic quaint, and sucks you backwards in time to become its little black-and-white bourgeois pets. It is very tidy, though. The TV is a big wooden console with this little bubble screen. Later in the evening, Dwight will turn it on, watch the green glow emerge from the center of the static pattern, start swearing like a stevedore because *Entertainment Tonight* is still squatting on Ed Sullivan's time slot. The Davis place is a museum of Modernist furniture; liberal use of avocado and autumn gold throughout. A spiky light fixture orbits above the dining room table like a little silver Sputnik. The air smells of pot roast, which is to say, like garlic and domestic surrender.

Sunday dinners here at La Casa di Davis are always meatloaf, or else pot roast. I wonder where Mrs. Davis even buys her pot roast. I thought pot roast went extinct during the Nixon Administration. It belongs in an exhibit in the Smithsonian, if the Smithsonian has an "Obsolete Cuts of Meat Wing." I honestly can't remember for sure. I went to Washington D.C. in eighth grade, but I was all hopped up on Dr. Pepper and thought I could see right through Cindy Scolari's clothes if I scrunched my eyes and deep-focused on the fabric, on the tiny spaces between the threads, using concentrated brain waves to make them widen out. I was a brown kid in a white school and I survived on a steady diet of such fantasies. So, subtract the frequent bullying, and that's about all that comes to mind from that trip: Dr. Pepper, migraines, big stone Lincoln slumped in his giant throne. I do recall that Big Lincoln had a look on his face like he was so tired and disappointed in all us puny, aimless sightseers from America's dim future. Just like the look Mr. Davis has going right now.

"What did you say you do again, Donald?"

"It's Durval."

"That isn't a Christian name, is it?"

"No sir, Indian."

"Mohican?"

"Manhattan, by way of Mumbai. My parents work in the tech sector."

"Oh."

"Me, I produce viral video advertising."

"So, what's that, movies about meningitis and stuff?"

"No sir. Viral meaning that they are widely viewed and shared electronically."

"Oh."

I am staring at Dwight's comb-over. I wonder how long it takes him to construct it in the morning. If, in a windstorm, it ever tears loose and whips around like a frayed tarp, putting out the eyes of innocent bystanders.

Mrs. Davis enters carrying two lemonades in cold, sweating glasses. She leans in and gives me one of those personal-space-buffer-zone hugs, the kind that means we're better than strangers, yet not friendly enough for actual physical contact.

"Hello Durval, so nice of you to come," she says.

"My pleasure, Mrs. Davis," I answer, "Thanks for the invite."

I like Mrs. Davis (call me Lorraine, she says, but I don't) and I'm never sure why. She looks like Diane Sawyer teleported six decades into the past, which is to say, like Diane Sawyer's grandmother. She's thin, sporting a red gingham dress and a haystack of blond hair that looks like it took several hours to tame. Lorraine Davis is a constant blur of activity, but most such frenzied people are active out of a love of activity; runners who crave that endorphin runner's high. She's active in a different way, a nervous way, like she's a runner scared of what slowing down might bring: old age, or being caught by an invisible lunatic killer.

"Here's a napkin for you," she says. I unfold it, to use it as a coaster. I quickly fold it up again, to hide the two words she's written on it.

Help me.

Later, after the pot roast has been reduced to scraps, I volunteer to help with the dishes, which garners me another Big Lincoln scowl from Dwight. "I suppose men do that sort of thing in India," he says, wiping his mouth and heading for the stairs that lead to the basement, which is actually a bomb shelter. Normal people would have spent the money on an in-ground pool.

Lorraine is waiting for me on the back porch, taking quick hits from a cigarette hidden behind her back and fanning the air with her free hand.

"Are you okay?" I ask.

"Hell no," she says. "I can't take this anymore. Can I go with you?"

"What? Go where?"

"Tonight. After the intervention. Please, I don't want to stay here with him another day, just drop me downtown. I'm already packed. I'll get a hotel room."

"Why don't you just leave anytime you want?"

She sits on the concrete step. "I don't know how to drive," she says, stubbing out her cigarette and wiping her cheeks with the back of her hand. "I have to walk to the supermarket every week. I lug the bags back, with all the neighbors watching. Isn't that pathetic?"

"Not for 1955," I say.

"Maybe you could give me some driving lessons sometime?" she asks.

"Sure, you bet."

"I like modern cars," she says. "Is it true that some have heated seats now?"

I nod.

"Do you think I'm too old to go to college?" she says, to no one.

+++

When we are all assembled (me, Didi, Lorraine, Didi's older brother, George, who's just driven up from Cincinnati), we head down the narrow stairs, single file, through the blast door. I go last, feeling my way, filming as I walk. I'm expecting some prime footage.

The lights are dim and wash the tiny room in bluish tint. I adjust the gain on the camera. Dwight lies in full-horizontal position, at one with his recliner. Nat King Cole croons softly from a spinning phonograph. Lorraine pokes Dwight's shoulder. He mumbles something about Eisenhower's French whores and snores awake.

"Dwight, wake up. This is an intervention."

"Huh, whah?"

"A final attempt to reach you. Or consider it your own personal McCarthy trial, how's that?"

"Goddammit, Lorraine, are you waking me up just to call me a Commie? How dare you!"

"No, you're a confused dictator, and we're here to make some changes. Starting with the calendar. Dwight, it's 2013, not 1955. Jesus, you weren't even alive in 1955. You were born in

Toledo in March, 1962. You missed the 1950s entirely."

"No," says Dwight. "No way. Not possible."

"Dad, it's true," says Didi. "Mom has a copy of your birth certificate."

"Bullshit."

"You remember anything from your childhood?" asks George. "Hippies? The Beatles? Civil Rights Movement? Do you remember watching the moon landing with your mom and dad? Or did you make them switch it off? When did you leave the real-time continuum? When did you take the Cold War and make it a permanent way of life?"

"I don't remember any of it," says Dwight.

Didi kneels in front of Dwight and pulls up her sleeves. "See these, Daddy? Do you remember when these happened? No, you probably don't. You were too busy sneaking down here to hide from reality to know that your daughter saw nothing but fat every time she looked in the mirror. I was fifteen. Did you know I used to lock myself in the bathroom and puke myself sore? Making little cuts was the only thing that helped. I felt dead inside, frozen solid, but the little red, oozing cuts, the stings, they always brought me back. Nothing could bring you back, though. It was like my dad's trapped alive inside this old picture on the mantel. But I'm real. This skin is real. Why can't you see me? Why can't you care about me?"

Dwight refuses to look at Didi's arms. He checks his watch instead. I don't focus on her arms either. Doesn't seem right.

"My turn," says George. "Hey Pops, do you know what happened last month? Get this—I married my boyfriend! I married Seth, out in Vermont, on the steps of the state house. Gays and lesbians can do that now, in 2013. What do you think of that, Dad? Does that blow the comb-over right off that petrified Fifties brain of yours? Good! You know what else we do, when we're alone? Want me to describe it?"

"Stop it, George," says Lorraine. "That's enough. This isn't family therapy. We can get into that some other time. This is about getting your father back."

"Back? Really? Is that what you actually want, Mom? Him back? Why don't you tell dear old Dad about the suitcase that you've kept packed and hidden in the back of the closet? How many years now, four? Five?"

"Not now," says Lorraine. Dwight looks up at her. She looks away. Dwight checks his watch again.

"What the hell was so special about the Fifties anyway?" asks Didi. "I don't get it."

"You wouldn't understand," says Dwight, red-faced. "None of you. A guy worked. He worked hard all day and when he came home, his wife was glad to see him and she handed him a martini like he was the engine of the family and they'd just been coasting along without him, empty under the hood while he was gone downtown working for the best government in the world, and his kids were glad to see him, too. They couldn't wait to tell him about their successes at school, how they'd say they were just trying to do their best to follow his example. The guy felt like there's no place else he'd rather be. King of his bungalow and lord of his half-acre. And all across America, it was the same; and where it wasn't, the Blacks and the Mexicans and the Orientals were saying to themselves, 'That's what I should aspire to! I want a martini, too!' and all the way on the opposite side of the world, the filthy untouchables wading in those Calcutta sewers were looking up at that guy and they could almost picture sitting in their own bungalow, if they worked hard enough, and what that martini must taste like. That guy was The Man. His wife would never think of going on trips without him. No daughters with eating disorders. No homo sons prancing around in public, disgracing the family name."

My cheeks turn hot behind my camera. Dwight sounds just like my father, minus the Hindi accent. It doesn't matter to either of them what I do, we do, it's never going to be good enough. They live half a world apart, those two, and yet they share the same empty opinion of their sons.

"Don't you people understand?" says Dwight, louder. "That guy had a limitless future once. You don't have to like him, but our nation was built on guys like him. A guy who sacrificed. He deserves your respect. He did his best. And if some girl he knew from the neighborhood messed up and didn't use protection and got herself pregnant, he had to step up. He had to scrap his big plans and make smaller ones. He did it because that's what people expected of him."

"God, I don't even know you," mutters Lorraine. "And now I've lost myself too."

"Fuck that guy," says George. "He's extinct. For good reason."

"You're wrong," says Dwight. "He's a hero, it's just that no one ever sees it."

"Like hell he is. I'm out of here. I need to get back home for work tomorrow."

"You're not going anywhere," says Dwight. "I am." He stands and walks to the door. "You've got thirty-six hours of oxygen in here, and some bottled water. Get cozy. Piss in the empties if you have to. You'll have a lot of time to talk about how you all despise me. How I've failed you. Just stay calm. The Fire Department will have you out long before the air's gone."

He stops in the doorway. "Most things went unsaid in the Fifties," he says, staring at the floor, "but it doesn't mean they weren't felt." He slams the door shut. We hear him latch it from the outside.

We don't know what to say to each other. Lorraine sits on edge of the recliner and cries. George fiddles with the door, bangs his fists on it, to no avail. The internal door release has been tampered with. Didi paces in tiny patterns. I sit on the cold concrete slab and concentrate on taking small, slow breaths. I hope Dwight is telling the truth about the oxygen supply.

Long minutes pass. An explosion shudders through the walls of the shelter. The lights flicker off then on again, spotlighting thin streams of dust falling from the ceiling. After that, it falls silent, for hours.

+++

Later, after the paramedics cut us out, after we are treated and released, while Franz is apprehended trying to cross into Mexico at the Laredo border station and the rest of us hold a five-minute memorial service for Dwight (who now fits into an eight-inch-by-eight-inch copper box), I finish my movie for Didi. I reframe it as a tribute to her dad, sort of a modern tragedy. It chokes her up. It's some of my best work. She still can't watch it all the way through. As of yesterday, it has about a million views on YouTube. My social media has blown up over it and suddenly I have this career that even my own father can't deny.

I kept the first half of the footage intact. After the intervention scene and Dwight's exit and our panicked quiet, Lorraine crying, George banging on the door, I fade to black. When the picture returns, I pan around the empty shelter, focus on Dwight's journal, his vintage album collection, the phonograph arm skipping at the end of the record, mindlessly spinning out static. I walk the camera through the door and up the narrow stairs and out into daylight, opening up into a panoramic shot across the smoldering remains of the house, the whole area cordoned off with yellow tape and surrounded by gawkers. Where various parts of the house used to be, I cut to corresponding old photos of Thanksgiving dinners, Christmas mornings, little Didi dressed up as Raggedy Anne for Halloween, Dwight and George hoisting George's first figure skating trophy high above their heads. I added a soundtrack to this part—Connie Francis singing "Who's Sorry Now."

After the photos, I walk the camera through the rubble. My free hand digs around, pulls out a tobacco pipe, wipes it clean.

With the final frames of video, I narrate a voice-over epilogue. I wrote it myself, using a few lines borrowed from his journal. I guess we wrote it together:

Dwight slams the door, throws the latch, checks his watch. 9:54 PM. He runs up the narrow stairs, switches on the porch light, dials the Fire Department and repeats the address, repeats the phrase "bomb shelter" over and over. He steps onto the front porch and sits on his lawn chair. He reaches under the chair for his pipe. It is a warm night, the smell of half-dead lilac next door on the breeze—the kind of evening front porches are meant for. Perfect weather for remote flying.

Some kids are gathered in a driveway down the street, dribbling a basketball and smoking. The sharp smell of pot. A rap song thumping from a car stereo. Dwight Davis closes his eyes and drifts, until the clock spins backwards and kids turn whiter and crew-cutted and the music sounds more like Bill Hailey and the Comets. Nighttime in summer in Toledo, Ohio; nighttime in America at the dawn of the Space Age, back before any drones, back when a man had plenty of privacy for the questionable aspects of his life, back when we first started launching hardware into the skies just because we could. Imagine that! We shocked the world. And sure, once in a while one of those machines would turn on us, a prodigal child, but that was acceptable. Failures sometimes fall back down flaming, just as they should. A nervous future is the price we pay for always being the first ones through the door of tomorrow. Abe Lincoln may have said that, before he saved the nation and freed the slaves and then got shot dead for his trouble. Maybe that's why he still can't manage a smile.

Rest in peace, Dwight MacArthur Davis. Even the coldest wars end.

Sunday Drive

Eastbound on Route 422, between SOM Center Road and 306, is where all the leavers go to do their leaving.

The grassy berm is uneven, swampy for stretches, overwhelmed in spots by stunted pines and scraggly oaks. In summer, cattails conceal things. In winter, the walls of plowed snow. It is April now, and windy, in between masks. Nothing hidden but the sun.

We roll to a stop on the gravel shoulder.

She takes my hand. She squeezes hard. We wade into the wash of things they've left.

Cardboard boxes of squirming kittens, threadbare couches, bloody weapons of choice, shredded bras, gigantic panties, plastic sacks of anonymous trash, personal belongings of exorcised exes, stained mattresses, ponds of reeking diesel, bald tires, broken mowers, aluminum deck chairs, an old cancerous dog.

Just past the Rest Stop Five Miles Ahead sign stands the white wooden cross. Stapled to it, a photo of a baby girl. Strung from it, garlands of plastic flowers. Wanted and not. Did but didn't. Someone planted this small confession. This is why we come, to learn what they knew. Many leavers are young, most are hurried, few linger, a mere handful return.

She needs some time. I wander back to find the old dog.

The old dog licks my hand, rolls over with difficulty, lets me rub his neck. His stomach is swollen fat with tumor. When he quiets, I hit him at the base of the skull with a rusted pipe.

I go to find her. I watch her carry a box of kittens in her arms, set it next to the cross. She covers them with panties.

She likes to visit the cross on Sundays. The earth here is soft. The clinic on Fourth is surrounded by concrete. Nowhere to dig.

See, this is what we should have done, she always says.

We're so much smarter than that now.

Forgetful Street

The street where I grew up was a forgetful one, Mom said to me, when I asked about the dad unable to find us. Real Dad, that is, the one with the Browns jacket, the one that smelled like leather. The other dads that came home to us from their various workplaces were different dads, stranger dads, smelling of new cars or shellfish or sulfurous blast furnaces. Dads that left grease stains on door frames and wiry black hairs in the shower drain. Dads who sneered the lights into flickering, who exhaled foreign atmospheres.

It went unspoken that the dads were not to be spoken to, but some spoke at me anyway, in beat-its and little-shitheads. Sometimes, a nicer dad stopped mid-wallet and said hey kid, here kid, and left me some cash as well, on the table, stuck under the edge of the ashtray.

Many of the dads made noises—howled like hungry beasts, pummeled the walls, yelled out haikus strung of filthy words—but once in a while, a dad preferred quiet, and crawled deep inside it and into Mom's arms and wept there like he was lost. Those dads reminded me of ghosts, and amnesiac dads wandering the earth crying out like ghosts, and those nights I went up to the attic and stuck my face into the box full of old shoes. On the nights of the loud dads, I stayed in my closet and counted my nice-dad-money by flashlight; money I'd need on the day I became a man and lost my memory and start going home to other boys' houses.

Mrs. Endicott's Boarding House for Men Formerly Lost at Sea

The man who occupied the Forsythia Suite in those final days of the boarding house, a formidable maelstrom of a man who absorbed and incinerated all goodwill within a mile's radius, a man who referred to himself as Benoit, or Benoit the Accursed (1981), was once again inebriated and throwing all the furniture out the windows of his floral-themed guest room and, in the process, had awakened Mrs. Endicott (the owner) and the other eight residents of her boarding house, each of whom had returned from the depths of the sea during the month of June—or rather, the last nine Junes belonging to the previous decade. And now it was that peculiar month once more; a warm night in June, 1986. The windows of the boarding house were thrown open as much as the early summer air permitted, to flush out the long winter's stench. Mrs. Endicott had learned this much: that the combined and lingering smells of brine and decay that attached themselves to a houseful of formerly drowned men was not to be underestimated.

"I won't go back!" Benoit screamed, lost in another waking nightmare. "Not down there!"

A few of the men had gathered on the lawn beneath his window, careful to watch for falling knick-knacks. "Calm yourself, Benoit!" they called up. "You're dreaming again."

Benoit stuck his head out of the window. "Fools! All of this is dreaming! The day is coming when you will awaken and you will realize how Benoit was correct! See to your own wretched bones, Brothers, and for God's sake, hide the liquor!" His head disappeared from view. Moments later, a rocking chair hit the ground and splintered, followed by a table lamp.

Mrs. Endicott used an old skeleton key and was soon inside the room with Benoit, surprising him from behind and caning the rabid Frenchman about the head and torso until he removed himself from the windows, grabbed a satin throw pillow and huddled in one corner, moaning, curled fetal, an inconsolable drunken baby.

Elliott (1980), the red-headed lobsterman, and the young German U-boat crewmen (Henryk, 1978, and Klaus, 1983) stood in the hallway outside Benoit's room.

"Need help with that one, Ma'am?" asked Elliott.

"No, he's reached his remorseful place," she said, heading for the stairs, patting the lobsterman's arm as she passed. "He'll be down in a few minutes with a 'pardon moi' and a 'je suis desole.' All will be forgotten by breakfast." Mrs. Endicott stopped at the landing. "But when I find out who's been sneaking him rum, there will be a reckoning in this house."

And the three men believed it.

Nine Junes had brought nine boarders and had filled Mrs. Endicott's house to capacity: McComber, ensign in Queen Elizabeth I's Royal Navy (appeared 1977); Henryk (1978); Trulgard the silent Norseman (1979), who was constantly followed by a flock of raucous gulls; Elliott the Maine lobsterman (1980); Benoit (1981); Voerdaans, the captain of a Dutch slaver (1982) who had tried one too many November crossings of the equatorial Atlantic; Henryk's crewmate Klaus (1983); a tall, dark-skinned African tribesman whose name sounded closest to Mogobydego (1984); and Crusty Jim Brundage, an obscure and failed pirate hailing from the Outer Banks of the Carolinas (1985).

Apart from the minor detail about the apparent reanimation of waterlogged corpses, it seemed a normal boarding house like any other. On Saturday evenings, Mrs. Endicott gathered the men in the parlor after dinner and poured out glasses of root beer, to stand in for rum or ale, and led the group in storytelling, followed by a sea chantey or two, perhaps accompanied by Voerdaans's concertina (because Mrs. Endicott had never learned to play the piano that stood neglected in the corner), and all of the entertainment (tales and songs) cleaned up and fit for the presence of a lady; i.e. no references to fresh young whores, seasoned old whores, whores of any size or flavor, pretty cabin boys, female genitalia, male genitalia, or gratuitous violence. "Hers" became their code word, though barely disguised, and Mrs. Endicott let it pass, so that a passerby might hear something like this on a warm summer night:

"Hers is the reason we set out to sea,

And hers is the reason it burns when we pee,

And these are the three things we know to be sure:

A sailor needs tailwinds and whiskey and hers!"

+++

Sundays were quiet and reflective, stealing past virtually unnoticed, like the first washes of high tide. On Sundays, the men were not permitted at the table for pancakes and bacon unless they'd already shaved, washed and put on decent clothing. The boarding house contingent took up two pews at Calvary Presbyterian, in the back-left corner, where it smelled vaguely of fish, and a long-dead sailor could nod off during a sermon without rebuke. McComber carried his own water-stained Bible, his favorite passages marked by dog-eared pages. Mogobydego pulled his sleeves down, to cover the scars from the wrist manacles, doing his best to ignore the bigoted stares of the all-white congregation. Trulgard stood guard in the back, massive arms crossed, his gulls settled over the roof of the church like a pulsating cap of snow. As usual, Crusty Jim sat on his hands when the collection basket was passed—a necessary precaution.

Overall, the men seemed to like church, as much as they liked anything, and perhaps a bit more. With the exception of Benoit, though, the men formed a sullen crowd, as if the life put back into each of them was but a sputtering flame, a mere candle-flicker of a normal soul's fire. Nevertheless, they seemed somewhat happy at meals, and when together in the parlor, and at church. Once, on a painfully cold Christmas Eve, the children's choir sang "Stille Nacht" entirely in German, and both Henryk and Klaus broke down and had to escape out into the snow to cry in private. The next morning, with a cold sleet pushing inland, Mrs. Endicott passed out hand-knitted scarves to the men, offering a special "Frohliche Wiehnachten" to the German boys. One by one, the men gave Mrs. Endicott trinkets they'd carved in their spare time, from driftwood or soap: penguins, seabirds, anchors, even a narwhal. Crusty Jim presented her with a necklace he'd stolen from the local jeweler, a show of extravagant warmth, but the spirit of the season got the best of him by afternoon and he went back to the shop the day after Christmas, in disguise, leaving his own prized pocket watch and chain on the counter.

+++

Before running the boarding house, before becoming the widow who visited Brietenbach's Collectibles once a month and met in secret with old Brietenbach Sr. himself, Mrs. Endicott was known as Margaret Mary McKinney, a rarity among Irish girls owing to her black hair and kelp-green eyes. She had come to Pequihasset with her father, Ian, dragged along behind as so much additional cargo, never intending to stay longer than it took to dry out her clothes from six weeks aboard a cramped steamer launched from the port of Galway. Ian McKinney measured three-fourths of a man at best, ever since the night his body was mangled by a plummeting anchor chain off Inishboffin. Measured in fish, Ian was more of a release than a keep—his career a patchwork of random, bone-grinding crew billets on cargo boats or fishing trawlers, laced together with frequent shore-leaves lost to alcohol and dice. In his lucid moments, he gathered all the good pieces of advice he never tried himself and carved them into his oaken left leg, so they'd be near at hand if he ever changed his ways. He told one thing to his only daughter: get yourself far from the sea, girl, because that bitch takes more than she gives. Go inland, where she can't reach you, Maggie. Go to Ohio, where the earth is soft and holds the dead up nice and high, so you can chat with them on Sunday afternoons.

As daughters go, or as the Irish go, she did not listen.

Ian frequented the same docks where Everett Endicott worked, tending to the family boat nine months of every year. Everett was a full five years older than Margaret. He was a local boy, ruddy and wind-burnt, a natural sailor who'd recently inherited his father's forty-five-foot outrigger trawler, the *Bonnie Marie*. He drank only tea with honey. All of this was enough to make Margaret stay in Pequihasset, years after her clothes had dried.

Upon her engagement to Everett, Ian McKinney bought every man in The Black Gull a round of Dominican sugarcane rum, and as they downed their shots, tried to slice their necks with a broken bottle. When he sobered up, he heaved his rucksack over his shoulder, signed on to haul net on a cod boat, and was never seen again. Ian had the curse of the sea, people said. Spend enough years with her, and the tide seeps into your blood. After that, she'll pull you where you don't want to go.

+++

Margaret Mary McKinney Endicott kept the box on the nightstand next to her bed, where she could stare at it in the dim light and dream of the things it might do. On that particular night, after Benoit had exhausted himself and the other boarders were asleep, just past midnight, she draped a wool sweater over her shoulders, pulled on her sealskin boots and headed out into the darkness, the box tucked beneath one arm and a lantern dangling from the other hand. It was now June the 21st, the summer solstice, and she would mark it as she had the previous nine years.

When she reached the spot where the Cobb's Channel Light lined up between the granite humps of the Two Sisters, which stood every bit of four miles offshore, she set the box down on the sand and opened it. The coin she pulled out felt cold and fat and heavy between her fingers. In one motion, she coiled an arm back and unleashed it low, the perfect motion she'd learned as a child for the optimal skimming of stones. The coin bounced once, twice, a third time, marked by ripple-births, until it stopped altogether and settled into a trough between two waves.

Mrs. Endicott walked home to the boarding house, wiped the sand from the bottom of the box, set it on the nightstand and tried to sleep. She tried to envision, even dared to hope for, the one she would most like to find in the morning.

As she often did, she imagined him grown. Her favorite image: he was tall, his skin blue-gray from years beneath the waves, young hermit crabs teasing their way through tangled hair, and a snarled beard grown thick in the depths, but with eyes of warm brown, and his nose and mouth unmistakably hers. She imagined it easily could be others, too, cheap replacements: ancient explorers, modern-day leisure boaters, either too old in age or else too old in era, missionaries, mercenaries. She fell asleep imagining most every man but the one she found.

He was there at daybreak, standing in a pool of saltwater trapped by the cupped and warped oak planks of her front porch.

Her own Captain Everett Endicott.

+++

The box had first come to Margaret Endicott this way:

Her wedding reception was held on the grounds of the Endicott Mansion, later to become the boarding house, on a late September afternoon when the leaves began to brew their color and the air dried and cooled, the first signs of summer gathering her belongings. Many familial branches and knots of Endicotts had travelled north from Massachusetts or south from Portland for the affair. Margaret, with no family anywhere near Pequihasset and a father wandered out to sea again, could not hope to remember so many strangers, so many names. There was Lionel, (Lowell?), the one who could have been Everett's older brother; a certain cousin Rosalie from Manhattan who'd been fired from some of the best shows on Broadway; the little twin girls from Boston, both names beginning with "E," one fat and one thin, like a baseball and bat.

And the old woman in green. The stooped crone had not given her name, and Margaret never asked for it, but the woman handed

Margaret a gift wrapped in sailcloth and kissed the bride's hand. "I have no more need of this, dear," she said to Margaret, "but you do."

The next day, while the caterer cleared the remains of the festivities, Margaret and Everett opened the wedding gifts. The last to be picked up, wrapped in sail-scrap and smelling of brine, was a wooden box, intricately carved. "This must be from your great-aunt," said Everett, smiling. "I didn't think she was going to make it through the ceremony. What is she, ninety-something?"

Margaret set the box down, drawing her hands back. "But I thought she was your relative!" she said.

"Never seen her before," said Everett. "Strange, isn't it?"

He picked up the box and opened it. Sand filled the bottom of the box, and nestled in the sand were coins of all types—small bars of silver, like small ingots, stamped with Roman numerals; oblong gold coins bearing the head of a Greek; smaller gold coins with the inscription "Felipe, El Rey;" others made of copper turned green with the patina of saltwater and age, square holes cut through them. Everett laughed as turned each one in his fingers. "I think that these," he said, "should remain in our family for a long, long time."

Margaret said nothing. She had learned too well from her father how the sea loved and hoarded its things.

+++

Everett sat at the kitchen table, clutching a mug of coffee, the warmth chasing some of the blue from his bloated skin.

"I'm sorry, Maggie," he said, gagging, spitting silt from his teeth, his first words formed in twelve years.

"For which offense?" she said, her back to him, arranging muffins on a plate.

"For taking Wallace out there," said Everett, pressing the cup to his forehead. "I knew you didn't want me to, but I thought it was time, time for him to start being a man. Learning the trade. I should have listened to you, Maggie. I never stopped to think that you'd end up alone because of it."

"But I'm not alone, Everett. Did you see how many have come? You're lucky there's one more bed left, up in the cupola. You can sleep there. Leave your dirty clothes at the bottom of the steps. I'll introduce you to the rest of the men at supper."

Everett, despite the wasted years he could have spent in preparation for this moment, could think of nothing further to say.

Margaret set a plate of peach muffins in front of him and went outside to tend the garden. There, kneeling amidst her tomato plants, she cried and pulled the suckers from the stems with her thumb and forefinger and tried to picture Wallace's face. Not the grown Wallace, but the boy Wallace, at the age she had last looked upon him. She could not. She tried to start with the grown Wallace and work backwards, peeling off the years back to childhood, but as the younger man neared boyhood, his face faded from her, features blurred in fog or salt spray. She stopped only when her knees grew sore. Half of her tomato plants had been stripped to the ground.

+++

In the evening, the men sat down to pot roast and mashed potatoes. They made room for Captain Endicott at the head of the table and gave the usual boarding house newcomer's welcome, peppering him with questions about where in the Atlantic he'd climbed up from, whom he may have seen, which wrecks he may have passed on the way.

Mrs. Endicott whistled for silence. The clamor subsided.

"I have a job for you boys," she said. "Nine of you will leave in the morning, to go look for my son. One of you will stay behind, to help me with the house. No stories or songs tonight, you all need your rest. Off to bed with you!"

One by one, the men cleared their plates and climbed the stairs to their quarters. They had all figured in their heads who the nine were, and who the one. The house grew quiet while Captain Endicott sat alone at the dining table, enjoying the lightness of dry land, the gentle pressing of air on a body used to the crush of fathoms. His half-widowed wife worked in the kitchen, packing nine sacks with the next day's lunch of fried chicken, green apples and cornbread.

It was eleven by the time Everett rose from his chair and retired to the cupola. His footsteps passed her room. Margaret sat on the edge of her bed, the box on her lap, waiting another hour before leaving the house. At midnight, quiet as a wraith, she felt her way through the gardens and down toward the water, not lighting the lantern until she was beyond sight of the house.

At the usual spot, she waded into the waves, clutched the box with both hands and heaved the entire thing into the surf.

+++

That night, wrapped in a blanket wrapped in a dream, Margaret's father came to her, his *slip-thump*, *slip-thump* along the wooden wharf unmistakable, even from a distance.

He looked younger, she thought. Happier, too, than he'd ever looked. His oaken peg was gone, replaced by a length of gleaming whale rib. He stood by her bedside, fingering the box on the nightstand like he'd held it before.

"Gave the old leg to the grandson," he said with a wink. "For all those sayings I carved, see. One a day, I tell him. Learn just one a day, boy, and you'll be the better for it."

"I miss you, Daddy," said Margaret.

"He's a good lad, Maggie," said Ian. "Pride of the sea, I tell you. And she loves him hard, too, something fierce. Holds him close to her, and won't let me stray far neither. Lucky as hell I stole this one chance to see you."

Margaret wanted to ask him what he meant, where he was, but it was already too late—her father had been found. A bouquet of barnacles burst forth from his mouth and spread out across both cheeks, and he could speak no more.

+++

The next morning, a Monday, was the quietest ever in the long history of Pequihasset.

Without the snores of fleet diesels in the pre-dawn, most of the town slept late, including Mrs. Endicott. Only when the sun warmed her face did she stir from her bed. She put on her housecoat and made her way to the kitchen. The nine lunch sacks were gone, as well as the three jugs of water she'd left on the counter.

Outside, on the front porch, Henryk waited. He touched her shoulder and pointed toward the shore, to where the ocean should have been, but wasn't.

+++

I could tell you about the journey of Captain Endicott and the other eight as they made their way past the fishing boats mired on their sides in mud and silt, down into the damp cellars of the sea, marching in a line, Benoit reciting a long list of the dangers they'd surely face, and Trulgard sending his gulls ahead to scout a path through the sharp ridges of damp granite and down the cliffs of the continental shelf. I could tell you of the wrecks they climbed through, calling out again and again for Wallace but finding only broken ship-wares and emptied casks, and the wrecks they dared not approach because they stood guarded by fields of the dead. I could tell you of the gasping mackerel the men struck against rocks and ate raw next to the last remaining saltwater pools, because there was no dry wood to be found for a fire, and of the constant stench of rot on the air, and of the shimmering hills of snow they saw from afar that turned out to be endless flocks of seabirds feasting on the carcasses of whales. I could describe the last days of the second lives of these men, but it is not their turn. This is not their story.

+++

For the third night in a row, Mrs. Endicott slid from her bed and made her way to the shore. She carried the lantern and a small shovel. After thirty minutes of dragging and digging, she found it, further from the former waterline than she had imagined it would be.

+++

Her bed was cold and her nightgown damp with sea mist. If all has gone well, she thought, from out of this darkness will come the sound. And then there it was, on cue: the sound— the one she knew so well. For as long as she could remember, Margaret Endicott had awakened at five in the morning to that sound, and to the start of another day, like all residents of coastal fishing towns. Out of the bowels of the very deepest quiet, one diesel sputtered and rumbled to life, then more, then many, as the whole fleet stirred, idled, then throttled up past the break walls of the harbor, heading to open water—the universal alarm clock of water-folk. But on this day, it also meant, of course, that the sea had returned.

Mrs. Endicott switched on the bathroom light. The mirror, as always, her too-honest companion. She saw the lines of her face carving deeper into her skin, lined up like waves, saw her years piling up around her eyes and the corners of her mouth like the flotsam of a winter's high tide, leaving few years remaining, while the greedy ocean still held endless wooden hulls and steel holds full of lost men and cargoes, still held Everett and her beloved son and the other six crewmen of the *Bonnie Marie* somewhere over the sharp drop of the Grand Banks, all but one of her recent boarders, her restless father, and countless others too, innumerable drowned strangers, a cornucopia of claimed lives to trade for her few precious coins, tens of thousands to send Mrs. Endicott in place of the only one she really wanted: her dear Wallace. There were simply not enough Junes left for her to find him; the cold laws of probability and time forbade it. And so that is how she decided, on June 24th, 1986, that her searching was over.

She told no one where she buried the box; not Brietenbach Sr. (although he begged her to), not even Henryk. Mrs. Endicott would never touch the coins again, never pass them on to another pacing widow or grieving mother of the coast, never again take on another boarder whose clothes were still damp from the depths. Instead, she would move Henryk to Ohio, where the apple trees grew as numerous as the dune grasses on Upper Pequihasset Beach. She would learn to play piano and tend a small garden and spend her last good years in the company of a son, even if it meant settling for a son borrowed from another mother across the sea, or stolen from the sea itself.

War Crumbs

For us kids, Memorial Day weekend was all charcoal grills and parades, and it meant that we'd be packing up the minivan and driving twelve hours from Ohio to North Carolina, heading for the shore, which also meant that Great Uncle Henry was bound to fall apart again at any moment. And by falling apart, I don't mean becoming overly emotional, breaking down, acting "dramatic." Great Uncle Henry wasn't like that at all. He was a simple man and fell apart the old-fashioned way—limb from limb, and torso into segments. Most times, we didn't even have the luggage emptied into the beach house before we'd get the panicked shout from Aunt Celia, his only daughter, who never got used to experiencing the temporary disintegration of her father. She'd pour herself another double Seagram's and chain-smoke her menthols and pace the salt-bleached deck while we young nieces and nephews mobilized and combed the beach, the leeward sides of dunes, the garden, the house, all for old Henry's parts—sometimes a hand down in there between the rows of grapevines, perhaps a foot exposed at low tide, or a section of pale belly-flesh nestled among the towels in the upstairs linen closet. It was not, as some might think, a horror. Revulsion amongst us kids was minimal, especially when compared to the thrill of the hunt. Finding Henry, even the larger pieces of him, was heroic and life-saving stuff, the makings of stories.

When the parts were all accounted for and rinsed of their sand and mulch and patted dry, Aunt Celia would arrange them all in Henry's bed, in appropriate order, and lock the door for the night. We would then be free to play Monopoly on the screened porch, or take flashlights to the beach to scare up the ghost crabs, or maybe light a bonfire on the bluff and roast marshmallows, but the One Rule was that we had to stay away from Henry's room while he was mending. I was in charge of enforcing this rule amongst the kids, since I was the oldest. I'd shoo them all to bed by ten, and the adults would stay up another two hours drinking beer and talking about Iraq and stock markets until they couldn't keep their eyelids open. In the morning, Henry would invariably be awake and moving before any of us, out the door at dawn to take Roscoe for his walk.

This was summer's start at the beach, year after year, until I was fifteen. That was the year that Aunt Celia had just about enough. She drove in from Virginia all blotchy and coughing up black phlegm into handkerchiefs, and you could tell that she had nothing left as far as Henry was concerned. She coughed up a lot of euphemisms, too, dubious phrases like "assisted living" and "quality care." Great Uncle Henry listened to her logic, but he wasn't the same after that. He didn't come apart at all that day, probably fearing that to do so would only hasten his departure. Henry spent a lot of time in his room. He offered no opinion, and Celia didn't ask for one; she wandered the Internet on her laptop, searching for local senior facilities. She asked me what I thought of some of them, the ones with the professional photos, and I think I nodded, but I didn't tell her that I could almost smell the piss and bleach right through the monitor. They looked like human parking garages, linoleum-lined stalls for families to store their older models.

The next day, I carried a glass of lemonade up to Henry's room and tapped my knuckles on his door. I told him it was me. He said to come in, and I found him sitting on the edge of his bed. He had a shoebox opened on the bed as well, and he reached inside it. He held up a chain, and hanging from the chain were two small metal plates. "Read them," he said. I said, "Thomas Gaynor, Sergeant, United States Army." I didn't read all the numbers. "That was your brother," I said. I had heard stories of Great Uncle Tommy from Mom, and she had heard them from her mom, Grandma Elizabeth, Henry and Tommy's sister, before Elizabeth died in a car wreck back in 1983. Tommy was legend; he existed in sepia, trapped in photographs that ended with him in uniform, his face a portrait of resolve that only heroes can summon. What I'd heard was that Tommy was two years older than Henry, but according to Elizabeth, anyway, they could have been twins.

"Tommy died in World War Two, at Anzio," I said. Somehow, I thought that. Maybe because I had seen a documentary once on Anzio and at the time, I thought I'd like very much to drive my own tank someday.

"It was Omaha Beach," Henry said in a tired voice, "and no, I didn't die there."

The ice disappeared from his glass before either of us could say anything.

Henry, or I suppose Tommy, ended the silence. "My brother Henry had this recurring dream that something bad was going to happen at Normandy. He saw soldiers crying with dozens of holes in them, like they were unfinished jigsaw puzzles, boys searching for their crumbs, and he made me promise that I'd look after Annabelle and their little Celia if he didn't make it back. He believed he was already done for. He stayed up all night, trembling, when we crossed the Channel. I tried to help him…"

"What happened?" I asked.

"I told Henry I'd be first off the landing craft," Tommy said, "so if the German guns were on us, I'd go down instead of him. But I didn't. Go down, I mean. All I remember is jumping, being in the surf, bullets screaming past, and then a shell's whistle and a concussion that knocked me face-first to the sand. I looked back for Henry, but the landing craft was gone, just pieces floating. Pieces of metal. Pieces of men. I started to pick them up, but the platoon leader grabbed my neck and shoved me to the sand. I left the pieces in the waves. I don't even know if they were Henry or not," he said, and just as he finished, his left elbow came undone and his forearm, hand and all, fell to the floor.

I went to pick it up, but he pushed me away with his other arm. "Go on, get out of here," he said. "No one should have to see this."

I ran down the stairs and over the dune path to the beach. It was high tide, so I had nowhere to stand but in the wash of the waves.

There were things beneath the water that tumbled past my ankles. It made sense now, I thought, his coming apart. It was the parades, the flags, the grayed and shuffling vets with their proud lapels full of medals.

When I walked back up the house, I gathered the kids together. "Special Henry-hunt today," I said to them. "Everyone bring the parts to me. Hurry!"

When I had a full rucksack, I slung it across my back and rode my bike south, fast, toward the cliffs that guarded the entrance to Manatauk Bay. I was the only one missing when Aunt Celia ran yelling out of the house, and someone else had to tell her to relax, that the hunt was already over. She became despondent, they told me, mumbling about purgatory sidestepped, or some such nonsense, and debts not paid.

Aunt Celia went to hospice herself, in 2004, due to the lung cancer, and for weeks she still wouldn't talk to me, because I wouldn't tell her where I put him. I never told anyone. But I don't mind giving you a hint, because you look like you respect the inviolate guts of secrets. The place I picked is close to the shoreline, and high up, just about impossible to get to without a rope.

I wrapped his parts separately, in plastic, so they would never grow back together.

When Celia's prognosis dwindled from weeks to days, I went to visit her one last time. I thought the truth, in this case, would be a gift. I told her everything Great Uncle Tommy had told me.

Aunt Celia made a sound like strangled laughter and shuddered so hard the oxygen tubes pulled out of her nostrils.

"What a crock of shit," Celia rasped, grabbing my arm. "So, he got you too, huh? Lying, falling-apart bastard of a father. And you, you little fool, you went and let him off the hook! Uncle Tommy died at Anzio. All the Army could find were his dog tags."

I think I shook my head no, but maybe it was just really wobbly at that point.

Celia couldn't talk any more, nothing but air came out, but she wasn't done yet. She motioned to me for a pad and a pen.

She wrote about Henry making it to the top of the cliff overlooking Omaha Beach. She wrote that they stayed there two days, nursing the wounded and rounding up German prisoners. Lots of mine fields, she wrote next. And then this: Henry's idea to make the young German boys march in front until there weren't any left. That's how he got through to Belgium, she scribbled. Stepping through their parts.

Celia didn't write or speak after that. She sipped oxygen from tanks until she died, three days later, on a Thursday.

The beach house sold for seven figures, to a plastic surgeon. We spent one last Memorial Day there, cleaning out the junk. Up there, in Henry's old room, fingering those dog tags, I made my decision.

I perched my body precariously on the ledge above the shoreline of Manatauk Bay. I barely had enough room to kneel and unwrap the pieces of his head and torso, arranging them in proper order. There was no room left for the leg parts. Those I took with me, back to the beach house. At night, I waded out with them and let the low tide pull them out to sea, no witnesses but the ghost crabs scrambling from my flashlight's beam.

I think about him sometimes, when I turn my thoughts to the weather. On cloudy days, I curse myself because I picked such a lonely spot, the sort of place where a soul would have nothing else to do but gnaw on its toughest remembrances. Other days, sunny ones, I know I did right, leaving Henry there with a view clear across to the sea-cliffs of France.

Farrah Fawcett, Guardian of Highway Bridge Abutments

The Monday morning I had given up all hope of ever finding you, I pinned a note to my shirt, swung the car into the outside lane, lined myself up with the I-70 bridge abutment and hit about 75 when the angel Farrah Fawcett appeared on my lap and stomped on the brake pedal. The car locked up, slid sideways into the guardrail, sparking metal grinding us to a stop. The air bag blew her into the back seat. I was covered in talc and side-window shards, a cut on my forehead but otherwise fine. Farrah was unharmed. She leaned forward and cradled my face in her hands and told me to be strong. Soon, she promised—like the first time she came to me, when I was maybe fifteen and she was wearing that incredible red one-piece and she snuggled in next to me in bed, under my arm, and I told her to be quiet, my folks were just down the hall. She just laughed, stroked my three-haired chest with the backs of her fingers and she said it would get easier. She'd help me. She promised.

But she didn't at first. For the next decade, I seized up around girls. My throat constricted and I couldn't talk right and the sounds that leaked out were pale and alien. I dropped books and spilled drinks. The more I liked them, the worse I crashed and burned. No matter, Farrah said, when she visited at night, they weren't right for you. They never were, so I buried myself in that mane of hers and cried until I swore I'd give my life over to her if she would find the right one for me. It's going to take some kind of woman to replace me, she said.

The Tuesday morning I had given up hope of finding you, I had my note and got into position when I saw an SUV with a flat stuck in the berm ahead, directly between me and the abutment. I slowed down and parked about fifty feet behind, put on my flashers, went to see if I could help. A graying old woman in a wool coat and scarf stood next to the car looking helpless. When I got closer, I saw it was no old woman, with no gray hair. My angel, teased Farrah.

The Wednesday morning I'd given up on life, I woke to find my car stolen. The cops found it five miles away, still drivable—no fingerprints, but a few long blonde hairs on the headrest. I took a taxi to the Columbus impound lot, looking out the window and listing all the new things I'd never considered driving my car into.

The Thursday morning when I got my car back, it was raining and I stayed in bed, buried in blankets. I imagined Farrah standing out there along the highway in the downpour, waiting, wondering where I was, her feathered hair getting soaked, hours of blow-drying wrecked by raindrops.

The Friday morning I swore would be my last, I was in position once again when the car a hundred feet in front suddenly swerved left and struck my abutment head-on, exploding in a cloud of metal and glass. I screeched to a halt on the berm and half of me was out of the car and running to help, but the stronger part held me motionless, watching the smoke sprout flames, waiting for the sirens. I didn't think Farrah would be permanently harmed, but she needed to feel something of what I felt—a singe or two, where it counted. But when I got back to my apartment, there she was, watching TV, the breaking news: a single young woman, thirty-one, had lost her life in a highway collision. I guess I'll have to start looking for another one for you, Farrah sighed. So sad. Come here and sit down, honey. Which I did, and I hated that I did. I wanted to be holding that young victim instead, pulling her from the wreckage, even smoldering. I wished Farrah had burnt in her place. I wished I'd noticed long ago that Farrah had no wings, and I wished that this wasn't going to end with me burning right alongside her.

The Night Driver (after Calvino)

Every night driver burns, aflame with a
need that sends them speeding down vectors of
pavement split into two lanes, thin yellow lines
slicing through the dead hours and sorting the
things they love from the things they hate, the
cold wind through the open window urging them
to stay focused; the rest is darkness and ceases to
exist; the music loud, escalating, headlights
reaching and sharpening, the coffee cold and
souring, tires pounding out rhythm on the joints
in the concrete and the rhythm becomes the
reciting of the things you hate, like when a person
promises to be your always/everything but then
after a while they cut their hair too short or gain
weight or lose weight or stop smoking when you
don't or change jobs and pretty soon their touch
is all wrong and they kiss like a Freudian slip and
their voice hits your ears as broken glass and they
start spending more time with other people and
you act like you don't like it but you have to
admit the absences do bring some relief. I hate
when these people pretend like this self-inflicted
distance is something that concerns them greatly
and they say they want to work on the

relationship and they enroll us both in activities like that wine appreciation class, which reminds me how much I hate wine-guys with perfect teeth and a shadow of stubble, wine-guys who say stuff like: a bottle of wine is a living being; a larva cocooned in a dark cellar, breathing, morphing, dreaming of the glass and the lips. I hate wine-guys who try to be poets and married women who drink it up. I hate when there seems to be some inside joke between those two, a joke that me and the living, breathing, naïve decanter of wine aren't getting. I hate that the wine-guy is a contact in our cell phones, and I hate cell phones that tell our secrets; they play at being secure but if you pick up your wife's cell phone when she's not paying attention and tap the screen quickly enough, before the screen locks, it spills all like a drunken friend which soon leads one to night driving, the twin lanes in perfect balance so you must also admit there are things you love, like cars—metal cocoons that take you wherever you want to go and let you writhe, never try to talk you out of what you're becoming and I love knives for a similar reason, they are born with singular purpose and don't try to be marriage counselors or divorce attorneys; they are simple creatures, whether cutting steak or resting on your passenger seat at night, catching and tossing the ghosts of passing streetlights, not dead, just sleeping, perhaps fitfully, dreaming of resistance and of pushing past, of separating things that should never have been joined in the first place.

Leave No Trace

The old neighborhood was nearly unrecognizable. The shake we'd been waiting for since winter had finally happened overnight, waking us from our restless sleeps, but the dim light of a few dozen wobbly stars had not been enough to illuminate whatever had been done to us this time. Not that it mattered much anyway; the simple act of our waking already meant defeat.

At dawn, we emerged from our stress-cracked shacks and tents and trailers (those that remained), rubbed our baggy eyes and wandered the streets, wherever there were streets. At places, the pavement stopped altogether, as if it had never been, and sometimes started again feet or yards away. It was the same for everything. Down by the river, Fisherman Frank's weather-beaten Airstream still stood, but the river that had passed just twenty feet from the door of his trailer yesterday now ended abruptly about a quarter mile upstream. The river was now more of a thin lake. If he lived, and if he stayed, Frank was going to have to hike to the water from now on. I could hear him swearing nearby, shaking his fists at the sky.

The center of town was in shambles. The Gathering House had vanished, along with the Californians' compound and all the garden plots that framed (used to frame) the south end of the square. In the center of the square, the old gazebo that was said to have survived four consecutive shakes (1975, '80, '85, '90) had not been able to escape the odds. Not even its outline remained. On the north end, though, the rock outcropping still dribbled out ground water that fed the basin beneath it.

All of the young maples that had sprouted around the gazebo since the last shake were gone, too, sucked below, so we sat and sweated in the summer sun as Mayor Ruth waited nearly two hours for the stragglers to trickle in from the border lands. Then she took a head count while Jimmy Numbers wrote on a scrap of wood. Four hundred twenty-one folks yesterday; one hundred and thirty-six today. Let us be joyful for those who are gone, shouted Ruth. She named them: all the Californians; Mitch Chicago and his three struggling, motherless kids; about half the opioid users from Dependency Village. There many others I didn't even know—maybe I'd seen them once or twice at the Barter Tents, trading their wood carvings for eggs, their extra carrots for socks. When she ran out of names, it was quiet for a moment. Then the wailing began in earnest. Those first couple days after a shake were always the worst. I remembered this from five years earlier. I can't even recall why I decided to stay back then. Maybe I'd been so lonely for so long that even life in this town full of slow-motion suicides was more human contact than I'd had in a long time, since Beth. Still, waiting to die was no way to live.

Joan Delaware was curled fetal on the grass. I went over to her and sat down and put my hand on her back for a while, feeling each heave of her sobbing. Joan arrived maybe two years ago, from somewhere out east. Delaware was just a guess. She was only forty-two, but slowly dying of some painful, wasting disease. Like most folks, she was not planning to be around after the shake. No one in New Madrid Springs made long-term plans. That was the whole point. The future had an expiration date of five years. This small dot-on-a-map town in southwestern Ohio was the destination for guilt-free endings.

+++

The area around the spring had been occupied for as long as history could remember, centuries before European settlers first laid eyes on it. The absence and then the presence of people on the grassy plain were the first threads of the fabric of New Madrid Springs, Ohio—as much as the red-bricked alleys in town full of idled migrant farm workers; as much as the whitewashed windows of vacant storefronts along Main Street and the town square's ramshackle gazebo that had leaned alarmingly to the east due to the prevailing winds. The spring that bubbled from the rock there had flowed for thousands of years, since the last Ice Age, the beating heart and the lifeblood of the small town that would take root at its feet.

Any folks that may have recalled the curious events of the summer of 1795 had long since passed on, leaving no one able to recall that New Madrid Springs was once known as "Rock That Weeps" in the language of the native Miami tribe who had hunted game on those lands for generations. It was there, in the center of the future town, at the natural spring, that the Miami resupplied their water skins each summer during the months of little rain, and it was there that Captain Jeremiah Nesbitt of the United States Army's 53rd Cavalry found the Miami tribe on the twelfth day of August, 1795.

Nesbitt was a counterfeit New England aristocrat and professional coward who had survived the Revolutionary War by managing to keep enough lower-ranking men lined up in front of him. After the war, he developed an accidental reputation as an expert Indian tracker, due entirely to the presence of his gypsy bride. She was a sorceress, some said—a dazzling raven-haired wraith of a woman who could appear as descendent from seraphim or sepulcher, depending on the lighting. The gypsy woman was childless, and had been unable to conjure any combination of elixirs and incantations which could reverse her misfortune. Each month, at the coming of her flow, she hid herself within her shrouded wagon and wept, taking refuge in her vials, powders, herbs, crystals, lenses, petrified bits of animals, and metallic instruments both wondrous and repulsive.

On that twelfth day of August, Nesbitt sat with Chief Talking Eagle of the Miami at the side of the spring and delivered the news of the Treaty of Greenville. All native tribes, he said, were to head north immediately, over the fertile country, to new lands set aside for them in the northwest corner of Ohio—swampland mostly, but Nesbitt kept quiet about that detail. The tribes were given two days to depart. Talking

Eagle left Nesbitt at the spring and directed his people to give the appearance of breaking camp, while Talking Eagle went off by himself to contemplate the slaughter of Nesbitt, and the devil woman, and the twenty-eight cavalry soldiers with them who were camped near the spring. Talking Eagle was a friend of Tecumseh, the great Shawnee leader, and he had already decided to join Tecumseh's confederacy of tribes whose sole purpose was to push back against the relentless tide of the whites.

That evening, the gypsy woman went to the spring to fill her silver basin and happened to gaze upon the first-born son of Talking Eagle, a handsome boy of thirteen summers, already as tall as a full-grown warrior, who had himself come to draw water. Her heart was at once full at the sight of the young man; its tendrils dove into the earth and up again at the boy's feet, where they entwined him and laid claim to him. Removing a small pouch from her coat, the gypsy woman ground the contents into dust within her palm, whispered a hex written in a tongue forgotten by the dead, and drawing a breath, blew the acrid dust from her hand into the wind.

The following morning, Talking Eagle awoke to news that his eldest son had been bewitched by the devil woman. The boy had been found by his frantic mother, standing motionless beside the spring, deep in some kind of trance. He remained that way all day, seeing visions to the north or else hearing voices that no one else could register.

Out on the grassy plain that night, a distant fire could be seen from the spring. The darkness had fallen strangely dense and black and silent, as if the world had been caught up inside a buckskin sack, and the chief considered that a good omen. The spirits and ancestors must be very near, he was certain—approaching across the plains, drawn toward his fire. He spread his arms wide. *Hear me, O Great Ones,* he called out over the sea of grass, *hear me tell of the devil woman's wrong, and breathe life into my words of vengeance. Destroy her and her demons. Rid our lands of their disease.*

Years later, the elders would recall that an anger awakened deep beneath their feet—a stomping and a snapping of rock, and the plains shook with rage in the darkness.

Dawn followed, slow and timid. The Miami found Nesbitt and a few members of his band scattered around the spring, their lifeless bodies crumpled in agony, their open mouths gaping. The rest had disappeared into fissures in the earth, some barely visible a dozen feet below, still being swallowed by the shifting soil. The chief's son was unharmed. He remained just as he was, expressionless and facing north, his eyes pointing the way toward their new home in the oak swamps. It was as if he had already seen that even Tecumseh's great confederacy of tribes would fail to deter the endless tide of white men and their wagons full of misery.

+++

Joan's sobs calmed. She uncurled and brushed her dark hair from her face. Her beauty was still there, but it was thin, a crust. We both knew it was crumbling away on the inside. She looked at me with those huge mahogany eyes, now shot with red and wet. Her voice was a croak. We're friends, right?

We were, but in the midnight moments when I was honest with myself, I'd admit that it wasn't enough for me.

I nodded, dreading the next part.

If I ask you to do something, will you do it?

I said nothing at first, because I hadn't made up my mind what I'd do myself until that very moment. I took Joan's hand and squeezed. Come with me, I said.

Where to? she whispered. I'm so tired.

I don't know, I said. Somewhere south, past Cincy, where it never shakes.

What would we do? I don't have much time left.

We'd get to know each other, I said. Are you even from Delaware?

No, she laughed, then coughed. I'm from New Hampshire.

See, that's something I didn't know. We could go on like this for months. What's your favorite book? Would you rather build your dream house on the beach or on a mountain? If you weren't so sick, where would you live right now? What did you want to be when you were eight years old?

Joan's face looked vacant, as if she'd locked up and left for a trip on the inside.

The Little Prince, she said, after many moments.

What? You wanted to be a little prince?

No, my favorite book. The Little Prince. "You become responsible, forever, for what you have tamed." I love that quote. I love it and I'm scared of it at the same time. Do you know what I mean?

Absolutely, I said.

You mean you love it, too?

I mean I'm scared by it, too. It's true. When you care for someone, it's like these thin little wires, these wordless promises tie you both to each other. Part of you feels constricted by it but another part of you feels like you're completely free because you feel like maybe there's a reasonable chance that you'll never be lonely again in this world. Have you ever felt like that?

She didn't answer. Her sickness was exhausting her. I helped her up and carried her back to my shack. I covered her with my blanket. She slept most of the day on my cot while I packed the few things I still had and re-connected the cables to my car battery. I tried the key in the ignition. The engine coughed, then caught. I turned it off and walked the half-mile to the remaining Barter Tents to trade my wool overcoat for some food. I needed to conserve all the gas I could. With any luck, we might make it all the way to Kentucky.

When I returned, late in the day, Joan was gone.

I drove around town as darkness fell, searching, stopping whomever I saw. I caught Frank heading back to his trailer from the thin lake, lugging his fishing gear. He admitted he'd seen Joan walk into the water and disappear beneath the mirrored surface, her pockets sagging, loaded down with stones.

I grabbed the old man by his shirt and shook him hard. Why didn't you stop her? I shouted.

Because tomorrow I might do the same damn thing! he spat, pulling out of my grasp.

I couldn't sleep that night because I was afraid of the dreams that would find me. I didn't even wait for sunrise. I drove south, not even caring if I drove into a chasm, and as the sky grew purple in the east, the pavement and the trees became less intermittent. By the time I reached Cincinnati, the earth's surface was unbroken and I wasn't even angry anymore. I pictured her curled on the silty bed of the thin lake. How long would she rest there? Five years? Fifteen maybe, before another shake erased the thin lake altogether, and with it, the entire existence of Joan Delaware. What freedom, to leave nothing behind! How long would I have to wait to feel that?

All through Kentucky, I drove on, thinking about what the rest of the survivors would do, those who had five years standing between them and the next shake. Half-ghosts, every one—not lucky enough or brave enough to vanish completely, haunting their half-selves.

The sudden realization struck me so hard that I jerked the wheel and pulled over to the gravel shoulder.

Joan had known all along that she was saving my life; that I'd never end my own while a gray shadow of hers or a silvered mirror-reflection still lived in my mind. As long as I was still breathing, so was she.

I wanted to imagine the thousands of other ways things could have gone, including the hundreds that would have had her sitting in the passenger seat next to me, wrapped in my blanket and asleep with her head against the window, but instead I kept coming back to the singular thought that she wanted alive.

She wanted me to live. It was evidence of something—of a responsibility, of a wire. It was everything.

What I'd Say to Your Tiny Miscarried Self

First—where the hell have you been, you little shit, I'd say, my voice a serrated shade of warm.

Then—my God, look at you, I'd marvel, you've got your mother's something and my something else; the details aren't important. Which reminds me, we saved that black and white image of you, the glossy grainy one that shows a white lump, with a larger white lump they said was your head, although we would have believed the opposite, too, so ripe to trust whomever, whatever.

I'd tell you it was a Wednesday afternoon when I found your mother deflated, smeared against the wall of the foyer, folded inward like a failed origami of herself. You would have hated that graphic silence, too, I think; tried to smash it open with whatever you could find, anything: begged a breeze down from upstairs, willed a slamming of the nursery door. The window of your room was left open to ventilate the fumes, the wind ruffling the loose ends of masking tape like November leaves, the room half-done in Sundrenched Yellow, patron color of prayers carelessly answered and of chicks counted pre-hatch.

Why did you go, I'd ask, but never mind that, it's just that you should have at least checked with me, first. If you were unsure, I would have told you to go to the ocean, right down to the waterline, to go find a conch shell and hold it up to your virgin ear so you could hear for yourself the haunted vacuum that treasures leave behind when they decide to go wherever it is they go, because then you would have come back to us saying so sorry, so selfish of me, I promise you both I'll stay, if you promise me you'll never speak of this again.

The End of Days Comes to Revelation Bible Camp

Back then, if you were fifteen, almost sixteen, and your mom decided on a bedroom-cleaning intervention and she went deep underbed and found the bag with the joints and the *Penthouses* and the boxes of shotgun shells (for your friend Metzger) that just happened to fall into your coat pocket in Aisle 7 at Outdoorsman's World, then it probably would have gone one of two ways. The normal route, favored by normal parents, would have involved groundings and chores and curfews; but then again, so what? You wouldn't be eating corndogs four days a week or making acorn rosaries or finding out the hard way that the redheaded kid in the top bunk was a late-blooming bed-wetter. The other route, the get-right-with-Jesus route, would have had your ass spending July right along with mine at a place like Revelation Bible Camp.

Back then, before the end came, you would have found Revelation Bible Camp sprouted from the remains of an old dairy farm in the far northeast corner of Ohio—the part that stays buried in snow from Thanksgiving through Easter—but during the remaining months, was one of the nicest areas ever overlooked by generations of westward-bound settlers. Not overlooked by the Amish, though. They found the climate just right for woodworking, and went and stuffed the whole county full of scraggly beards and cheese barns.

The camp bus was nicknamed Lazarus, because Old Man Beechum brought it back from the dead every May. It shuddered and spewed oily black smoke and was mostly populated with church youth group kids, gung ho knee-prayers, and bead-fondlers, the kind that chanted Yahweh Yes Way! when they caught their first glimpse of the camp sign, while me and a handful of other hard cases protested with Metallica on our Walkmans. I was the last one off the bus. Reverend Willis, the camp director, gave me the cold eye. He looked like an anemic prophet trapped in an Ohio State sweatshirt. The banner slung above the bus drop-off said The End is Near.

+++

The first morning of camp was Walk on Water time, where the campers lined up behind the diving board, and one by one, we were told to stroll out nonchalantly and step right off the edge into the deep end like we were headed into the arms of the saints. If you came up treading water, you swam to the other end and were pronounced a Watersafe Sinner, which meant you got to skip swim lessons. Others, like me, sank and flailed and were yanked up sputtering. We Sinking Sinners got handed a red wristband and a swim lesson schedule. When it was all over, Reverend Willis picked up a megaphone and said show of hands, how many walked on water? No one budged. Then he said, well now, if Jesus isn't one of you people, then I guess we still need to work on finding him, don't we?

Reverend Johnny Willis, as I would come to learn, had started out as Private Willis in the jungles near Laos, then spent the next fifteen years as Sergeant Willis, Purple Heart Willis, self-institutionalized Willis, homeless Willis, drunk homeless Willis, recovered halfway-house Willis, telemarketer Willis, relapsed Willis, and after having finally scraped bottom somewhere between telemarketer and relapse, became evangelical born-again Willis. No one who met him doubted his love of Jesus, but they always questioned his arsenal, so he wandered the Midwest until he stumbled upon a gig as chaplain at an Amish retirement home near Ashtabula. There, he bought a dark hat and grew a nasty beard and learned to build gun cabinets without power tools.

Reverend Willis told us this story at the Bible Camp welcome address: a struggling child of God befriends another struggling child of God named Simeon Yoder; sits at his bedside, listens to his stories, over and over again, rubs lotion on his cracked bunions, brings comfort to his final days, presides at his burial service, and then one day gets a call from a lawyer in Cleveland who tells him his was the only name on Yoder's will and so congratulations, Willis, you proud new owner of 375 acres in prime dairy country! There's your mysterious ways, campers. Somebody give me some amen.

If you were a troublemaker like me back then, and you still wanted more dirt on this Willis, and you were to give Old Man Beechum the camp maintenance guy some of the porno you packed in your duffle bag, he'd put down his toolbox and tell you the rest of the story, starting with a dayshift housemaid named Martha, whom Willis married. Plain to the eye she was, like human oatmeal, and a bit gimpy in one leg from a childhood buggy accident, but she was quiet and steadfast and gave him two daughters before God decided to reclaim the first. Girl fell down a hole or some damn thing, mighty strange if you ask me, and boy them were some dark, dark days that followed. Beechum would have told you about the frigid Wednesday in November when Martha decided to go after her and swallowed nine patients' worth of pills, leaving the Reverend and his other girl and his old guns and his new bottles on a plot of land big enough to absorb the tirades. Willis was no Job, Beechum would say, no siree, and then he'd pick up his toolbox and tuck his new porn under his arm and head out somewhere whistling "Just a Closer Walk with Thee."

+++

They put me in Tribe of Judah cabin. The cabins were plywood shelters with screened windows, grouped together in threes and scattered throughout the trunks of the oaks and white pines. The Amish guys that built them were probably disgusted by the plywood, but then again, they probably had them all built in twenty minutes or less. There were twelve of them total, named for the twelve tribes of Israel. Judah was located alongside Benjamin and Levi. The girls were together over on the other side of the chow hall. They got all the funky cabin names like Gad and Issachar.

Weeks dribbled by. I grew sick to death of Amish hymns and corndogs and badminton. I was sick of Christian Trivia Bingo Night, and of whittling little apostles for the Reverend to sell at the turnpike truck stop. I was sick of all the girls that would talk to me, and had no chance with the rest. But I really applied myself at swim lessons. The instructor was Willis's daughter. He never said her name, and she didn't either, but she could swim like a dolphin and had most of the Bible memorized. Everyone called her Nun behind her back. I tried not to, because she was dedicated to helping me out. Because of her, I made Watersafe Sinner by the end of Week 3. I asked Nun to do me the honor of cutting off my wristband.

+++

The bulletin board said Friday night, July 28th, the second-last night of camp, was the Annual God-given Talent Show and Parable Slam. I don't know why I took it so seriously— the grand prize was just a tie-dyed T-shirt with big black lettering on the front that said WWJC? Below that, in smaller print, Where Would Jesus Canoe? The back simply said Revelation Bible Camp, New Canaan, Ohio, 1985. I started writing down some ideas. My first draft sucked. It was about this starving apprentice fisherman who was trying to catch a fish to go along with his bread, like to make a sandwich or something, and the master fisherman told him that the only way to catch a fish was to use that bread of his as bait.

But the apprentice refused to do it; he was dead set on having that fish sandwich, and so the silly apprentice died of hunger, adrift in his little wooden boat, a sunburnt corpse covered with gulls that pecked at the bread clutched to its chest. I balled it up and fed it to the campfire. I needed serious help.

Nun was lying in the hammock on the front porch of the chapel, lost in First Corinthians. I felt sorry for Nun. She was actually sort of good-looking, in a subtle way, the way you wouldn't ever see dead on, but might catch one day out of the corner of your eye. She deserved better than the teasing she got, and certainly deserved a better set of circumstances. So much loss in her life, and now her dad, the Reverend, could only manage to tolerate her. He bore her company like a scar, a scar from the day something dearer was carved out of him.

I cleared my throat, so as not to scare her, and said Hey, could you write me a parable? Please? and she said, I've got to write my own, and I said Please again and she said About whatever I want? and I said Sure, and she said Okay, if you do something for me. She told me what the something was. I told her that something was something I could do. She went back to reading her scripture.

Here is the parable she wrote for me, the one I never got to read out loud, and had things turned out differently, the one that probably would have won me the shirt:

Suppose there were a certain man and his wife who had two daughters. One day, a band of marauders approached the house where this family lived, and forced them to their knees, and held swords to their necks, and demanded one of the daughters.

Which daughter? the couple cried, how can we make such a choice? Pick one yourselves, if you must.

We will take the daughter you love most, the marauders said, for they were most cruel marauders. Show her to us.

The father hesitated, then motioned toward the youngest girl.

The marauders laughed, called him a liar. They grabbed the eldest daughter, and fled, leaving the remaining three untouched, sentencing them each to one another.

+++

With that parable stuff moving ahead on schedule, I started thinking about the God-given Talent Show. I had a knack for just one thing, and that was stirring up the shit, and I figured that if God had bothered to saddle me with that, he probably meant for me to use it, and who was I to let him down? I considered my talent. I considered the favor I owed Nun. The two began to converge.

The big evening rolled around. Reverend Willis had his white collar on, and his drunk on, too. He reeked of sacramental wine. Nun was cutting squares of Rice Krispies Treats and doling them out onto paper plates. The special needs kids were all in a line up front, as usual, but Willis was in no shape to notice that there was one more wheelchair than there should have been. I had talked Timmy Dobeck into swiping the camp's collapsible wheelchair, and so there Timmy sat, closest to the podium, acting as special as the rest, which was no mean stretch for him.

Outside, the rest of the gang waited behind the rhododendrons. Pfister and Longrich and some of the other kids from the Tribe of Benjamin cabin had ransacked the storage closet where the Nativity Play costumes were kept, just like I told them to do, and they had swiped a few angel outfits, plus the ox head, and the donkey head, too, which I had subsequently covered in Elmer's Glue and pillow feathers to look like a misshapen eagle, maybe one of those raptor-rescued ones that flew into the grille of a semi. To top it off, Pfister found us a bonus box marked "Daniel Skit," complete with lion suit.

Reverend Willis tapped the microphone. Dusk was falling fast; time to get the show underway. Right on cue, Timmy started flailing and making a bunch of noise and screeching Beelzebub, Beelzebub. Willis stumbled down from the podium and put a hand to Timmy's head and said Out you go, foul spirit, and as soon as Willis touched him, Timmy flew out of the chair and jerked around like a marionette and sang I'm free, Oh God, free at last! Willis staggered back and thanked the Lord Almighty and everyone cheered and then something came over Willis, something scary, and he lunged forward and got into the faces of the special needs kids, one by one, and shouted for the evil legions to come out and sprayed their cheeks with his spittle until they cried and rocked in their chairs and started smacking their helmets with their fists.

I felt bad for those kids. That whole part was unforeseen, so I jumped ahead to Phase Two and banged on the glass and up popped the gang in the shrubs. I grabbed Willis by the back of the shirt and said Look Reverend, look, and pointed out the window to where one ox, one lion, one stupid eagle, and a pair of crooked-winged cherubim were staring back in at us. The lion waved. The ox smacked him upside the mane with a hoof. Lion put his paw back down.

At that point, if I had known Willis was going to totally lose his mind, I would have definitely hidden those kerosene cans.

Willis started tearing at his beard and wailing about the rapture and the four beasts and the seven seals and Come Lord Jesus Come. Then, just like that, he stopped. He started grabbing all the kerosene for the big Tiki torches and muttering how they would never be seen in all that tree cover. With two cans in each hand, he ran outside. We ran after him.

Reverend Willis climbed the ladder to the roof of the chow hall, stripped naked, and started dousing his clothes and the roof shingles with kerosene. Pretty soon, the flames were shooting ten feet into the sky on both ends of the roof, while nude Willis danced around in the middle of the conflagration and waved his arms over his head, calling down the archangels by name. One of the counselors dialed 911.

I grabbed Nun's wrist and we fled out around the back of the chow hall, stumbling over roots, twigs lashing our cheeks, down the path to the Sea of Galilee, one last time.

+++

The Sea of Galilee was a lake, really; spring-fed, cool, and clear down to pebbled bottom. There was a swimming area roped off at one end, complete with trucked-in sand beach, and the other end was stocked with fingerlings and left wild, for canoeing and fishing; just a boathouse and floating dock poking through the sycamores that lined the shore.

Nun and I sat on the dock and waited for the echoes of sirens. It was quiet enough to hear her stomach noise. She'd been too busy working to eat. I handed her a couple packs of saltines I'd swiped on the way out. She chewed. I thought about going home, and then I wondered what was going to happen to Nun, then decided that that was nothing I really wanted to think about. I said Hey, I never got to hear your parable. She reached into her shorts pocket. She unfolded a paper and read to me by flashlight:

One day, two children of a minister were sent to work in the milking barn. The elder, the favored, always did as the father told, and the younger, as no one told. The younger, bored, put down the feedbags and said to the elder, Come with me, to the abandoned farm next door.

They threw rocks at brittle windowpanes, howled the pigeons up and out of the roofless silo, carved bad words into the barn timbers and guessed at their meanings. The younger showed the elder how to jump up and down on the springy wood that covered the pit outside the barn, but didn't say which boards to avoid, and with a splintering, the elder fell through. The younger one laughed, because she had seen the filthy water at the bottom of the pit, but below the surface of the water lurked unseen things, things she couldn't possibly have known about, sharp things that could rupture spleens and collapse lungs. The elder bled and cried and called out for help. The younger asked, Will you tell Father that it was an accident? The elder answered, I'll tell him the truth. The younger asked this again and again, until there was no answer. On her way back to the milking barn, the steers laid down in the pasture, and it began to rain.

She started folding the paper back up, but I grabbed it from her trembling hands and balled it and threw it to where only the carp could get it.

You never wrote that, I said.

She said she needed to confess it to someone.

You just did, I said. Now it's done, Sara. Forgiven.

She turned and grabbed my shoulders and said what did you just call me?

Sara, I said again. I had known her real name for a few days, from the duty roster on the wall of the chow hall office, but until that moment, I didn't think that I had earned the right to speak it.

She cried and bit my lips and almost sucked the tongue from my throat. My hands found her bruises. Her hands took charge. We did it right there on the dock, quick and clumsy, ripple-birthing, kneecap-splintered, mosquito-assbit, and when we finished, I wrapped my shirt around her and we saw the one-thousand stars that had spread out over us while we weren't paying attention. Such tiny pale witnesses, each staring mute from its own far-off corner of nothing, and it was then that I remembered I knew a few of them.

Show me, she said. Say the names.

Look, there's Rigel, I said, pointing, right at the bottom of Orion the Hunter. And that's Betelgeuse, up on his shoulder. And that one there, go left from his belt, right there, that's Sirius.

Tell me again, she said, and I did. Mist tendrils rose and bats careened off things unseen and smallmouth bass popped for bugs on the surface. A loon called out, wanting just to be found.

Betelgeuse, Sirius, Rigel.

Don't forget their names, she said into my chest, it's all they have. Say them again.

Betelgeuse, Sirius, Rigel, I said again, louder, and when I did, damn if they didn't look brighter or redder or closer. Or maybe it was just the way all the other nameless ones were burning out, falling silent, learning what it was to be forgotten. But certainly, in the named, there was something.

Closer, softer, definitely something.

Breezes swirled our bare legs and shivered us both. There were voices now, still a way off. Flashlight beams lacerated the darkness up on the ridge, long fingers reaching downward. Dogs barked.

Betelgeuse, Sirius, Rigel, Sara, I said into her ear, and we waited for them.

Acknowledgements

I thank the entire crew of Tortoise Books for believing in this collection, and for their book-birthing expertise. I'm proud to join the team. "Slow and steady wins the race". Special thanks to Jerry Brennan, captain of the ship and my guide throughout the process, and to Leanna Gruhn, insightful editor and fellow Clevelander. They helped me make this book better than I thought it could be.

Many thanks to the editors who originally published many of the pieces from this collection in their wonderful journals, online or print: Michael Griffith, Jac Jemc, Chris Heavener, Lauren Becker, Kirsty Logan, Helen Sedgwick, Yasmin Belkhyr, Chris Tusa, Ross McMeekin, Tara Laskowski and Guest Editor Didi Wood, Christopher Anderson, Jenn Monroe, Colin Meldrum, Anne Trubek, Robert James Russell, Jeffrey Pfaller, Andrew Keating, Christopher James, Randall Brown, Ian Chung, Roxane Gay.

I thank John McNally, Porochista Khakpour, Geeta Kothari and Man Martin, who all told me I could do this, back when I needed to hear it.

My thanks also to the worldwide short-fiction community for your Internet-based friendships and your years of support and encouragement. There are far too many of you to name. You are legion and you are wonderful.

I thank Debra Eichelberger Palermo, who enjoyed reading and discussing my stories as much as I enjoyed her photography. She would have loved to read this collection but was denied the opportunity. I'm saving your copy for later, my friend.

A tip of the hat to my home state of Ohio, "the heart of it all." Ohio is like that weird uncle with the cheesy moustache and outdated clothes; the one who always has the best stories.

Special thanks to my graphically talented sister, Maggie Kapitan Burgan, for her assistance with the cover design, and to the three fantastic writers who agreed to blurb this collection: Ethel Rohan, Sara Lippmann, and Alex Pruteanu.

As always, I thank JoAnne, Luke and Claire, my favorite writers.

Publication History

Caves of the Rust Belt / *Hobart*

Letter from a Welder's Son, Unsent / *Midwestern Gothic*

A Sort of Theology / *PANK; reprinted in "A Pocket Guide to North American Ghosts" (Eastern Point Press)*

Pancho / *Corium Magazine*

Small Engine Repair / *Belt Magazine*

Mr. Forecloser / *"A Pocket Guide to North American Ghosts" (Eastern Point Press)*

Brothers of the Salvageable Crust / *The Cincinnati Review; reprinted in the Lascaux Prize Anthology 2014, as finalist*

What We Were When We Drew What We Drew / *Fiction Southeast*

Assisted Living / *Winter Tangerine Review*

Terms and Conditions / *Spartan*

Armored / *Annalemma; reprinted in "A Pocket Guide to North American Ghosts" (Eastern Point Press)*

Excerpts from Melrose Mobile Entertainment's New Carnival Worker Orientation / *Midwestern Gothic*

Mr. Yard Sale / *Cobalt Review*

Tiny Fake Us, Staring Out to Sea / *Jellyfish Review*

Fossils / *Fractured West*; reprinted in "*A Pocket Guide to North American Ghosts*" *(Eastern Point Press)*

Sunday Drive / *Journal of the Compressed Creative Arts*, reprinted in "*A Pocket Guide to North American Ghosts*" *(Eastern Point Press)*

Forgetful Street / *Eunoia Review*

War Crumbs / *A cappella Zoo*; reprinted in the anthology *BESTIARY: The Best of A cappella Zoo's Inaugural Demi-Decade*

Farrah Fawcett, Guardian of Highway Bridge Abutments / *SmokeLong Quarterly*

The Night Driver / *Journal of the Compressed Creative Arts*

What I'd Say to Your Tiny Miscarried Self / *Eunoia Review*; reprinted in "*A Pocket Guide to North American Ghosts*" *(Eastern Point Press)*

The End of Days Comes to Revelation Bible Camp / *Bluestem*

About the Author

Joe Kapitan writes from a glacial ridgeline located a day's march south of Cleveland, Ohio. His short fiction and creative non-fiction have appeared widely online and in print at wonderful venues such as *The Cincinnati Review, a Cappella Zoo, PANK, Smokelong Quarterly, Hobart, Wigleaf, Midwestern Gothic, Necessary Fiction, Belt Magazine,* and *Notre Dame Magazine.*

His first collection, *A Pocket Guide to North American Ghosts,* won Eastern Point Press's inaugural prose chapbook contest. This is his second collection of fiction. He is also sporadically at work on a novel in which he kills off his main character on page one.

When not writing, Joe Kapitan is busy in repertory as husband, father, licensed architect, war veteran, college football fan, recreational cyclist, petty philosopher, chief firewood-splitter and dedicated craft beer taste-tester.

He can be reached at joejoanne@sbcglobal.net, on Facebook and LinkedIn, and he is @joekap64 on Twitter.

About the Book

The natural successor to Sherwood Anderson's *Winesburg* collection, *Caves of the Rust Belt: Ohio Stories* travels to the Heart of It All, where drowned sailors reminisce over a hot meal and the rules of the yard sale are law. In his stunning debut, Joe Kapitan captures the modern Midwest in devastating detail, often blurring the lines between reality and the surreal. The depth of each story leaves readers wanting more as they dig into the pages of this remarkable collection. Memories of another America encase families like a Cold War bunker, forcing characters to confront the pasts that haunt their future. A man tries to renovate the exterior of an old mansion, but even in the state where All Things Are Possible, it is impossible to remove the cracks in the foundation and exorcise the ghosts in the basement. A school shares a message of resilience and community, while masking terrifying truths that appear all-too-possible in our current age. Kapitan has created a fantastical representation of the post-recession Midwest, presenting an image of a world where sinkholes don't just swallow the neighborhood, but also unearth hidden hope lying beneath the surface.

CPSIA information can be obtained
at www.ICGtesting.com
Printed in the USA
JSHW032212260821
18224JS00001B/21